THE BOOK OF JAKARTA

The Book of Jakarta

EDITED BY MAESY ANG
& TEDDY W. KUSUMA

Part of Comma's 'Reading the City' series

First published in Great Britain by Comma Press, 2020.

www.commapress.co.uk

A CIP catalogue record of this book is available from the British Library.

ISBN: 1912697327
ISBN-13: 9781912697328

This publication has been supported by the British Council.

The publisher gratefully acknowledges the support of Arts Council England.

Contents

CONTENTS

Introduction

JAKARTA IS A SINKING tropical megacity.

The capital city of Indonesia – the largest archipelago in the world with over 17,000 islands and home to 260 million people – will likely see most of its northern districts completely submerged by 2050. Although the effects of climate change and rising sea levels are visible across the world, Jakarta is sinking faster than any other city on the planet. Decades of unplanned development and excessive groundwater extraction have caused the land to subside by about 15 centimetres each year. As a result, Jakarta is struggling for survival. And yet, at a time when you would expect there to be a halt on further development, more and more buildings continue to go up, and people still flock to the city from other regions, lured by the promise of a better life – or simply to survive. Activists and concerned citizens are still campaigning tirelessly for change to help curb the impending environmental disaster, while the government announced that it will be moving its capital from Jakarta to East Kalimantan – nearly 1,250 miles away – in the not-so-distant future. Jakarta is truly at a turning point; the future of the city and its inhabitants uncertain.

Indonesia is a relatively young country, in which over

the last 75 years Jakarta has established itself as the political, cultural and economic centre. The city is where Indonesia declared its independence in 1945 (after years of Japanese occupation, and prior to that centuries of occupation by the Dutch and shorter periods by the Spanish, British, French, and Portuguese), and embarked on its never-ending journey of nation-building. Jakarta witnessed first-hand the rise of the longest dictatorship in the country – President Suharto's New Order – which was characterised by Machiavellian developmentalism that left a long trail of severe human rights violations and the exploitation of natural resources in the name of progress. The city is also where this regime met its end when four university students were shot dead while protesting, igniting a bloody wave of riots and racist hate crimes that eventually toppled the New Order in May 1998. Back then, the promise of reform seemed possible; Indonesia shifted to a decentralised approach of governing, saw freedom of expression improve, and the nation readied itself for the first direct presidential election in its history. After the initial euphoria faded, however, it gradually became clear that the country, and indeed Jakarta, hadn't quite rid itself of some of the darker aspects of the regime. Twenty years after the reform, activists are still being detained, oligarchs have a stronger grip on key resources in the country, and more and more citizens are fearful of expressing themselves in public due to increasingly oppressive laws.

As well as a political hub, Jakarta has long been at the centre of Indonesia's literary scene as it was where most publishing houses, media outlets and cultural organisations established themselves and flourished. Consequently, Jakarta-based writers dominated the literary landscape, which was in part shaped by the short stories and writers published in literary magazines and national newspapers. That said, censorship was rampant during the New Order; the government banned over 2,000 books and persecuted hundreds of writers, artists, and cultural activists for being critical of the regime. As a result, short stories published in this era often use symbolism and surrealism to bypass the censorship and deliver subtle social critiques. The reform in 1998, coupled with more widespread internet use, ushered in a more creative era in which a wider variety of stories emerged, as well as publishing platforms. While in the past being published in a national newspaper was the epitome of success, many contemporary writers chose to experiment, publishing their work on blogs, community forums, or social media, reaching new readers in the process. Today, as more literary festivals and publishing initiatives emerge in cities like Makassar, Padang, and Yogyakarta, the literary scene is slowly moving in a much-needed and more diverse direction. Yet, Jakarta remains an important part of Indonesian literary life and a source of inspiration for writers that have called it home.

The stories in this collection are written from a variety of perspectives, exploring the experiences of everyday life in Jakarta from all angles; the tricks and manoeuvres people use to survive and thrive in this chaotic city. The characters gathered here are not those in power, the decision-makers and politicians, but rather those on the periphery who feel the consequences of political, social and environmental change in deeply personal ways; people whose stories are rarely captured in the media. They remind us that there is no one way to see a city or experience an event, whether it be communal conflicts or personal crises. The stories of contemporary Jakarta are the stories of tricksters with many faces, wounds, and triumphs. Such is the spirit embodied in the ten stories selected for this collection.

The events of May 1998 marked a peak in racial tensions across the city, when riots and sexual violence targeting Chinese Indonesians took place and went largely unpunished. The wounds that were created, and deepened, by these events remain unhealed today, as is reflected in some of the stories gathered here. Cyntha Hariadi transports us back to this time of unrest in 'The Sun Sets in the North', a story exploring class differences within Chinese Indonesian communities from the perspective of two school girls whose friendship doesn't survive the riot. Hanna Fransisca's 'The Aroma of Shrimp Paste' is an account of a Chinese-Indonesian woman trying to navigate a bureaucratic nightmare in an immigration office, illustrating with humour how long it takes to make political promises a reality. In 2019 – twenty-one years after the fall of Suharto – students took to the streets for another pivotal protest against the government to hold them to account for breaking their promise of reform after 1998. Sabda Armandio writes about this second wave of unrest in his story 'The Problem' from the perspective of street buskers in West Jakarta, making us question whose narrative we read when we read a story.

Jakarta is a city that is struggling to contain its own growth, and as a result, an overwhelming number of Jakartans spend most of their days out on the streets, on their way somewhere. In 'A Day in the Life of a Guy from Depok who Travels to Jakarta', Yusi Avianto Pareanom follows a middle-aged suburbanite on trains and in taxis, malls, and coffee shops as he runs one errand after another, only to realise that he'll have to go through it all again the next day. The characters in Ratri Ninditya's 'B217AN' take us on a motorbike ride through the city, passing skyscrapers, abandoned construction sites and narrow alleys, while reflecting on the anxiety and restlessness of young, middle-class Jakartans trying, in their own ways, to resist the mind-numbing effect of life under capitalism.

Other stories explore the growing frustrations caused by city-wide development and expansion. Dewi Kharisma Michellia's 'A Secret from Kramat Tunggak' is set against the backdrop of a closed-down red-light district that funded many of Jakarta's first major developments, a part of the city's history that it would rather forget. Class tensions within the city's art community are explored in Afrizal Malna's story, 'All Theatre is False', set in the government-owned art complex Taman Ismail Marzuki, and Ben Sohib's tragicomedy, 'Haji Syiah', spotlights the different groups within the Betawi-Arab community of Jakarta. Together these stories challenge any attempt to present a singular narrative about any one group of people in this intensely diverse city, that is home to hundreds of different ethnic groups from across Indonesia, each speaking their own dialects, as well as the national language, Bahasa Indonesia (from which these stories have been translated).

Some writers chose to set their stories in a future version of Jakarta: 'Buyan' by utiuts imagines a sunken city in which technological advancement fails to negate the impact of the climate crisis. While Ziggy Zesyazeoviennazabrizkie writes about Jakarta as a ghost of its former, radiant self after it is no longer the capital of Indonesia, and the helplessness of people who lived their best years during the city's transition.

All the writers in this collection have called Jakarta home at one point in their lives, but, as you can tell from the range of themes in their stories, they vary widely in terms of background and style. The book features established names whose work has won literary awards next to those who hone their craft in Jakarta's alternative poetry community. Some writers started their career through short stories published in national newspapers, while others never chose that route to publishing, opting to share their work through blogs and online forums instead. Their stories are made available in

English in this book by translators who themselves have strong ties with the city; seven of them being Indonesian, actively challenging the notion that we do not translate our own stories.

The work of curating and editing is messy, slippery, and always imperfect. It is an impossible task to accurately represent a city, with all of its multitudes and complexities, in ten stories. No matter how thorough or well-intentioned editors are, we are bound to neglect important perspectives and fail to amplify crucial narratives. With this caveat, we hope that you treat the short stories featured in *The Book of Jakarta* as an intriguing pit-stop in your exploration of the vast archipelago of literary works about Jakarta, and Indonesia as a whole.

Maesy Ang & Teddy W. Kusuma
September 2020

B217AN[1]

Ratri Ninditya

Translated by Mikael Johani

TOMORROW I'M GETTING MARRIED and tonight I rest my head on your shoulder. You swerve your scooter around these alleys as if you know their ins and outs like the back of your hand. The further we go, the less I know where we're going. Doesn't matter, I think. I want to go even further. The narrower the alley gets, the more room to drown myself in. Rows and rows of tiny square houses. Every now and then, a cigarette stall. A badminton court sans net – the rubbed-out lines smack of desperation. The sound of a boy reciting the Qur'an blares out from the mosque's speakers. Other boys scream and run away from their mothers, not wanting to go home just yet. A brown river snakes on my right, sometimes narrowing, sometimes widening. A snack wrapper is trapped between two rocks, the current not strong enough to drag it away.

'We have to go the long way, the main road is impossible to get through.' You sound happy, as if nothing has ever happened between us. Last night I sent you a text, *I'm getting married in two days*. I waited for your reply until I fell asleep. This morning you said you wanted to take me to a seafood stall in the suburbs. I also live out in the suburbs, but on the other side of the city. If we don't cut through the centre we will have to go around the outskirts, through these narrow alleys. I think that's going to take ages, but I say yes, let's go. It's better that we end this without a fight. This afternoon you picked me up at the usual spot. One angkot[2] ride away from my house, an internet café that's now being converted into a shop selling phone top-ups and used mobile phones. When you arrived, the only thing you asked me was did I bring a raincoat, it's going to bucket down soon. 'I brought my poncho,' I said. Those were the only three sentences that have come out of our mouths since.

I wrap my arms tighter around your waist. I can feel a stiffness in your back as you try to sit up straighter without saying a word. I lift my head and move my arms behind me. A woman picks up a dress that has been drying on a fence, a baby cradled in her other arm. Our eyes cross. The baby screams when she sees me and the woman stares at me as if I'm a person with no soul. Or maybe this is all in my head. In these awkward seconds, I try to smile, but it must look more like a grimace. I try to look straight ahead, watching the road. In my peripheral vision, I can see her eyes following us until she's out of sight.

Forty-five minutes later, as if we have just fallen down a hole in a pinball machine, we arrive in a totally different landscape. A huge field stretches to the horizon right in front of us. No more asphalt. Only sporadically placed, gigantic pillars of reinforced concrete. An abandoned toll road development? I feel like we've lost our way, but I don't want to ask anyone for directions, as suddenly all the little voices that have been banging inside my head for the last few months sound as if they're finally being muffled. In this strange place, I feel like I can do whatever I want. There are no rules. Nothing is ever wrong. Because I've already forgotten who I am.

I remember the last time I felt like this. I was with you, too. We were in your room, watching *American Psycho*. We had just met that day – thanks Tinder! I lost a bet with my friend, and since I didn't have any money to pay him, I'd agreed to download the app and go on a date with the first person who liked my profile. I saw your picture and I thought you looked quite sensible. I met you at a minimarket, and after we drank our coffee you invited me to go back to your place. Even now, I'm sure that wasn't your own room. The place must've belonged to your friend who'd gone away on a holiday, and you'd asked him if you could use the room to fuck girls from Tinder. While we were watching the movie you said, 'Imagine if Patrick Bateman was on Tinder, hahaha!' I laughed along with you, hahaha. 'Patrick Bateman is a hero for corporate slaves like me.' 'That's true, he's like the Batman... though he'd be better off as the Joker! Hahaha.' We laughed and laughed and you began to kiss me, and I imagined someone finding my head in the freezer the next morning.

What really happened the next morning was not quite as bad, though perhaps a little out of the ordinary. There was another woman lying there right next to me. Her face so close to mine. I had no idea how long she had been watching me sleep. She smiled, stroked my hair and kissed me. I was worried I had bad breath, but she didn't seem to mind. Maybe because she also had bad breath. I started fucking this woman and you were right next to us, watching us with hungry eyes as if you were watching the Asian Food Channel. The woman left and then I did it with you. You were copying the girl's moves. I thought, next time I should do it with two men.

Later that day I went back to my usual routines and I'd never felt so trapped. I did my tasks at the office as I always did but the world started closing in around me, suffocating me. Which was weird as I worked in an open-plan office. I thought, *I should call you again.*

Screech! Our scooter gets stuck in the mud. I get off to help you lift it. There's no one else here so the two of us have to do the job. Luckily the puddle isn't too deep and the scooter isn't too heavy. 'Are you alright?' you ask. I nod my head. We hop back on the bike and continue on our way, past an enormous telenovela-style mansion that stands proudly among the rotting concrete pillars.

Sometimes I imagine you will rot out here on the streets. As far as I know, you never finished uni. You live like a bum. You never tell me what you do for a living. But whatever it is, it looks like you're doing it because you choose to do it, not because you're forced to. Sometimes when I think about that, I get angry. People like me have to study really hard to get into the best school, the best university, and then get the perfect job that promises a better life. Sadly, this middle-class manual doesn't have a chapter on how to feel content.

We had a fight once about this at a noodle shop. When you get angry, your eyes never pop out of your head, you never scream, you just get even more sarcastic and laugh even harder. 'People go to university to learn how to become the perfect servant for a glitzy multinational corporation. Haha. Fishing out turds from the Ciliwung River is still more dignified than wiping those white people's arses. You think their arseholes are plated in gold? You expect to find gold nuggets in their shit?' The instant noodle soup with the extra corned beef and cheese in front of me now tasted like a pile of shit. I am not one of those kids with parents who set up trust funds for their children and grandchildren so they can choose whose shit I have to clean up. 'For me, being able to live like a bum is a privilege. I can only do it when I have money. The best I can do is to become a mediocre employee,' I said. You went silent for a moment and then laughed even harder. You said everyone had their own cross to bear. I looked at your collarbone sticking out of your shirt, how can you bear your cross when you look so fragile? I said I'd always felt that all the things I possessed since I was a child had been stolen from somebody else. But I was too weak-willed to return them to their rightful owner. And now people around me steal even more things from me — yes, those fucking expats. And then we went silent again for a very long time.

On our next date, you told me all about your life. Your parents owned an oil palm plantation in Sumatra. They sent you to school in Jakarta. You were used to the good life, so you wanted only the best things: skipping classes, hanging out at the uni canteen, getting drunk all night, going to massage parlours, looking for girls to fuck. Years sped past and you left the prospect of academia for life on the streets. You got sick of your friends who were full of radical ideas but when they graduated started working at jobs that allowed them to think they were making themselves rich when what they were really doing was impoverishing other people, and themselves, at the same time. You started hanging out with factory workers, slumlords, and people who minded the stalls near the factory next to the university campus. Sometimes you worked as a parking attendant when your monthly stipend ran out early because you spent it on gambling with the scooter taxi drivers. One day you got into a fight with other parking lot attendants who accused you of stealing their spots. They gave you a right old bashing behind the milk factory. You nearly died. But you were more hurt by them screaming at you that you were a thief just like your mum, dad, and ancestors. A random accusation that just happened to be true. A woman who worked at the milk factory found you and helped you. You became close to her, you might even have fallen in love with her (you didn't give out many details in this part of your story). You shared your views about life with her. But she said she could not fully understand you, just as you could not fully understand her. One day she was gone. She never tried to see you again.

A drop of water falls on my arm. The rain gets harder. You step on the gas and ride towards a broad avenue, leaving the huge field behind us. Traffic quickly gets worse after it rains. I can feel coolish water from the gutter on my ankles.

We stop next to a cigarette stall to put on our raincoats. You offer me yours, it's more waterproof. I refuse, 'It's too suffocating for me.' You laugh, 'So many things suffocate you.' After buying a pack of cigarettes from the stall, you say we should light one up before we get back on the scooter. 'My bum's starting to hurt.'

A single bar of neon lights up the whole warung.[3] Your face in the rearview mirror as you park your bike; a strange expression, halfway between exhaustion and disappointment. I've never seen that side of you. To me, you always seem happy, contented, even when you recite to me your tales of woe.

I sit right at the end of a bench, under a tarp roof. My phone rings. It's my soon-to-be husband. I hurriedly pick up his call, so you don't have to look at his face on the screen or read my nickname for him. You move towards the bench to sit down. I stand up and walk away. I don't want you to hear me speak to him on the phone.

A drop of rain falls from your forehead to your cheek. You look like you're crying. You're starving and your belly makes a noise. You smile and laugh. 'We're nearly there.' The warung owner asks where we're going. 'The seafood stall next to the train tracks,' you say. 'Oh, I thought that place had closed down. Be careful on your bike, looks like it's a proper storm.'

We smoke another cigarette and hop back on the scooter. The road under heavy rain is a proper battlefield for us riders. Everyone wants to hurry home, find shelter, slip under the covers with their partner. My trousers are soaking wet. My belly also makes a noise, but not because I'm hungry. 'Getting rained on on your bike is the saddest thing in the world,' I say to you. You reply before I even finish my sentence, 'Hahaha. Double the sadness for me, then.'

The seafood stall is located a bit away from the tracks, at the mouth of a tunnel, lit by the soft light of old naked bulbs. The tunnel is an underground disco – literally – with a disco ball that lights up bits of concrete the patrons have turned into makeshift tables and chairs. Next to the tracks before you reach the tunnel you can see tiny rooms made of plywood. Multicoloured Christmas lights hang over the door frames. You grab my hand and we stroll through the disco tunnel. The girls' eyes are on us. Their dark purple lips and cute hotpants. You tell me this is a dead end where broken train cars are left to rot. The whores who used to hang out next to the main rail track all moved here. The seafood stall has always been here. I think a plate of shrimps is a good idea before going dancing.

The stall is busy, the staff are many, huge woks and grills everywhere. A stocky trans woman is singing 'Like A Virgin' for everyone. She gives you a wink, you reply with a nod. We choose an empty table, with our soaked clothes and jumbled feelings inside our chests. After ordering a grilled baronang, battered calamari and boiled clams, you ask me, your voice like air, 'So where did you find the white guy, Tinder? What do kids use now, Bumble?' You have a smirk on your face, it feels like I'm being slapped. I nod and light my cigarette, pick up my mobile phone and show you his photo. 'Are you sure he's not Patrick Bateman?' You're about to laugh. 'Not funny,' I say. You're a corny dangdut[4] song, I imagine you saying this with your emptied out expression. This is all in my head. I am projecting my own idiocy into the emptiness in your eyes. I don't care what you're thinking. I just want to end all this without a fight.

I'm getting upset. Lucky our food is here, just before I begin my rant. Soon we're busy with the dishes we ordered.

'Do you come here often?' I ask you once I've calmed down. You think for a second then answer with a little hesitation, 'I used to, but back then things were very different. Big Girl wasn't here.' You point to the singer. 'But you know her?' I ask. You raise your shoulder and carry on eating. Not long after, Big Girl stops singing and comes over to us. 'Haven't seen you in a while,' she says to you. 'Who's this? Dora?' She points at me, then introduces herself, Big Girl, owner of this seafood stall, named after her. A long time ago, she used to walk past this place every day, but never came in to eat because she had no money. She would walk right past, though sometimes she'd stop because she loved the music playing in the stall. One day Big Girl's eyes met the stall owner's eyes. Madonna's 'Like A Virgin' was playing on the stereo.

His name was Laksono. He was a handsome man, but his face was haunted by a deep sadness that moved to the beat of his favourite songs. The music spoke to the world about who he was, and who he was Big Girl loved with all her being. She fell in love with Laksono. Laksono found out Big Girl liked the songs he played on his stereo. He took her inside the stall and they sat at one of the tables. He ordered food for her. They talked all night long. And every night after that. Laksono told Big Girl all his life stories. Big Girl told him all her stories, but never her real feelings. Laksono introduced her to the whores from the dimly-lit stall next to his seafood place. You can fuck any of them, he told Big Girl, man, woman, up to you. I'm bored with all of them. Big Girl refused the offer. One day, Laksono's stereo stopped working. Big Girl was afraid she would have no more excuse to continue her conversations with Laksono. She gave him an idea: what if he hired her to sing at the stall. She wanted to learn how to sing 'Like A Virgin' for Laksono and sing it every night for him. She could only do Madonna and dangdut songs. She would sing 'Like A Virgin' as an encore, or as a treat if one of the regulars asked her nicely.

'Where's Laksono now?' I ask Big Girl.

She said, curtly, 'Till death do us part, and it did.'

After we finish talking to Big Girl, the rain stops. And then you take me to the disco. 'Let's experience a real underground party!' We share a beer and then walk around checking out the multicoloured lights on the whores' stalls. They go blink blink blink. 'Let me take you home once the beer settles down.' You take my hand in yours again. We sit on the pavement and light our next cigarette. 'I thought you and I were thieves stealing from each other. Turns out you were just waiting for bigger prey.' Tears rain down my face and drop on to the wet asphalt. I can hear ambulance sirens, engine sounds and car horns in the background merging with the sound of my weeping. Sitting next to this railway track I feel so alive but also so far from life. I'll never be able to escape my own pretensions. The version of me that I like the most is the version when I'm with you, I say the words in my heart. You tap my shoulder, time to go home. I ride pillion again on your scooter, heading towards the main road. Slowly the version of me that I like the most will fade away inside the broken alleys of this city, inside its cigarette stalls, inside Big Girl's seafood restaurant. So slowly you don't even realise it, like when a traffic gridlock just begins to unravel. But I've lost something even bigger. We ride slowly past a giant advertising billboard that was uprooted by the storm and now covers the road. Two bodies are smashed under it. I see a blackened ankle and a broken collarbone. Big Girl's silhouette appears before us, surrounded by neon lights and the blinking disco ball of the tunnel disco. She winks at us seductively, daring us to turn around.

Notes

1. The title of the story, B217AN, takes its inspiration from a typical vehicle registration plate in Indonesia – the B stands for the region, Jakarta. The title is also a pun on the phrase 'berdua satu tujuan' (together one destination), which is a popular joke among people who are always on the road.

2. Angkot: a mode of transport which falls between a taxicab and a bus.

3. Warung: a type of small family-owned business – a restaurant or café – in Indonesia.

4. Dangdut: a genre of Indonesian folk music that is partly derived and fused from Hindustani, Arabic music and to a lesser extent, Malay and local folk music.

The Aroma of Shrimp Paste

Hanna Fransisca

Translated by Khairani Barokka

A FICUS TREE GROWS in the yard of the immigration office. Unlike ficuses that grow in cemeteries, or in the central city squares of Java, there is no cool breeze wafting from its leaves. Perhaps the Jakarta heat is no longer compatible with the might of the ficus. Or is it the dry, and slightly frightening, immigration office that makes the breeze from the ficus tree feel the opposite of cooling?

It's underneath that uncooling ficus tree that a hangout spot for street food vendors has formed, for a gang of cigarette-smoking hustlers, for men and women who are prospective overseas migrant workers and seem to be having a rough time of it, and for many other humans – some in uniform, some not – sweating while drinking iced water.

You couldn't even hope for a bird to rest on that ficus tree, in the immigration office yard. And in the main street, before entering the worn gate, as usual, the cacophony of Jakarta's big roads does your head in. The riot is godawful: the roar of exhaust pipes, horns beep-beeping, the shouts of driver's assistants, and whatever sounds from humans of whatever sex, always just making a din.

This morning, I was picked up by the service bureau that sorts all of one's passport needs. 'Right up to the passport arriving in your hand, Ma'am. Everything sorted, guaranteed!'

insisted the man who didn't want to be called a hustler, and was prouder to refer to himself as an 'office employee'.

I could actually have sorted my passport myself. But because I was pressed for time, and a jillion things to do suddenly popped up, I had to use a service bureau, and be accompanied by an 'office employee' who was occasionally annoying.

'Ma'am, you aren't like other women, who are only 34 years old and already look mumsy,' said the office employee man, intending to seem friendly.

'You may be 34, Ma'am, but you still look like a 24-year-old girl. Honestly, I often assist women your age, they're usually fat and talk too much. Not like you, Ma'am.'

The hell. Then the office man added: 'Ma'am, you're very pretty. Not like in the photo.' And he finished it off with this closer: 'Hehehe.'

This lebaran[1] holiday, I'd gotten really lucky. I'd suddenly received a work bonus of a ticket to vacation overseas, plus full accommodation at pretty good lodgings. Since I didn't want to pass up this golden opportunity, I was willing to take a shortcut for a guaranteed passport with the price of one million rupiah, compared to the official, state-set price: two hundred and seventy thousand rupiah. The bureau guaranteed that the client wouldn't need to know the complicated process involved. And as an honest shortcut-taker would, I firmly said: 'As long as I get everything sorted.'

And then I was only asked to wear a white, button-down shirt, and to bring my official Family Card, official Citizenship Card, official Birth Certificate, and official certificate proving Indonesian citizenship. The main thing is that everything had to be official. 'Except for me, who could be an unofficial Indonesian, who'll be made official with a citizenship certificate,' is what I told him, and the office man rushed to reply. 'That's not what I mean, Ma'am. All the people of Chinese heritage who've become Indonesian citizens are automatically official. You just have to prove it, by bringing an Indonesian citizenship certificate that's really, *really* official.'

So here I am now, nine o'clock in the morning, with an 'office employee' man who appears to be some sort of overlord.

We're in front of the worn immigration office building, having parked the car not far from the ficus tree. Why am I saying that this office employee man seems like an overlord? Because as he's passing the ficus tree, many groups of men greet him with respect,

'Good morning, Mr Oleng.' That's when I find out that the overlord man has a funny name: O-l-e-n-g. And Mr Oleng, observing my reaction as many men gathered by the ficus tree greet him with respect, instantly says: 'They're just hustlers, Ma'am. Without offices. They run wild, and most of them are looking for prey in lost Overseas Migrant Workers.'

'OK, I believe you. As long as I get everything sorted.'

'Of course, Ma'am. Here's the deal, let's go inside.'

Good god. So many people are sitting on long benches. So many counters. So many officers behind glass, who at times speak loudly through round holes. I should feel like I'm entering a bank. But for whatever reason, I feel like I'm entering a train station. And those long benches are full of stranded passengers.

'Please sit down, Ma'am. Here's the deal, Ma'am. Whatever you get asked, just give short answers. So it's over quickly. When you're asked who's sorting these papers, Ma'am, you can just say my name, Mr Oleng. They all know me well. Wait here a little while, Ma'am.' Mr Oleng straightens his suit and walks towards the photography room. His hand waves to someone behind the glass.

'Hey, how come you're wearing a white button-down, Ci?'[2] a Chinese woman sitting to my left asks. 'They said no white button-downs. I was told to change my clothes.'

13

She looks at me full of confusion. Showing her long, purple eyelashes and blue, tattooed eyebrows. The curve of those eyebrows is as sharp as the cartoon character Sinchan's.

'Oh no! Seriously, Ci? I was told by the service bureau sorting my papers to wear a white button-down.'

'I don't know about that, how come the rules are different? I was told *not* to wear a white button-down, so I'm wearing a red button-down. By the way, how much did it cost you?' she asks, twisting her corn-like hair, spread across her shoulders.

'A million.'

'So it wasn't expensive. Mine was a million five hundred. I actually already have a passport, I just forgot to notice the year. When I was going to use it, turns out the passport had already expired. I just found out the other day, so I had to grab a shortcut. I'm leaving for a holiday in Europe, day after tomorrow. And during the fasting month like this, usually government offices close up early. That's why it's so crowded and expensive. Tomorrow's the last day, you know, if it's not sorted today, you have to wait until after lebaran. Hey, by the way, you're looking for work overseas, aren't you, Ci? In Hong Kong the prospects are better you know, compared to Taiwan. My friend told me the other day, they said the wages for even domestic workers are…'

'Madam Tjhang Chai Ha! Madam Tjhang Chai Ha!' my name is heard, called out over and over. The Overlord scrambles to come over and signals that I should quickly go to the photography room. Good thing I didn't choose the wrong bureau. The proof being that I only needed to wait ten minutes and can now be seen earlier than those who've been waiting for hours. How wonderful it is to be an honest shortcut-taker. You don't need to wait for ages, you can just zip right along. I look over at the girl who'd been chatting her mouth off, her face instantly soured.

14

I walk inside the room. There are several tables and cameras there. Each being guarded by a uniformed officer, busy point-pointing at each face they're going to photograph:

'Not upright enough! A little to the left! Sort that hair, don't let it cover your ears!' Bla-bla-bla, as hectic as a no-charge picture-taking studio.

'You want a photo taken wearing indecent clothing like that?' the officer in front of me suddenly barks.

'This is a government office, Ma'am. Please leave and come back here with long pants. This is a government office and everything's by the book.'

I'm startled.

'Well, what's the matter with what I'm wearing, Sir?'

'You're wearing shorts.'

'What? Don't you just need to photograph my face?' I still haven't realised that my question could complicate things. The camera officer is offended. His scant moustache suddenly begins to twitch.

'I am asking you to please leave, and to change into long pants, understood?'

'Gosh, sorry, I do apologise. Can we… just talk about it, Sir? I'll give you extra via Mr Oleng, the person helping me. Honestly, if only Mr Oleng had told me about this rule, wow, honestly I've been careless. Can you help me, Sir? I didn't bring long pants.'

'Sit over there! Straighten up!' he orders curtly. His spotty moustache, my god, it makes him absolutely undignified. He immediately photographs my face, silently, not seeming to care if I'm ready for the shot or not. Then he holds my fingers one by one, and only lets go when the fingerprints are recorded on the computer screen.

'If you would please leave, Ma'am, and discuss this further with Mr Oleng.'

I return to the waiting room and sit in my original spot.

I begin to get slightly anxious, looking to the left and to the right for Mr Oleng. What now? The Chinese woman who'd been sitting next to me has been replaced by a middle-aged man.

'Have you gotten your picture taken? You just need to wait to be called by the counter over there,' the kind man pointed to a counter, seeming to have guessed my predicament. I feel a bit relieved.

'Are you still waiting to be photographed?'

'That's right. It's been almost two hours. It's really outrageous.'

This whole waiting room seems to be filled with sour faces. The television is squawking with various news items, for who knows whose consumption. The TV can't be heard so well, thanks to the riot of mouths chattering from every corner. There aren't any newspapers for a casual read, no magazines as there would be in private offices. For the umpteenth time I feel as though I'm at a station, waiting for an announcement that the train has been delayed, which will be heard god knows when, and may or may not be audible. What's for sure is that Mr Oleng is nowhere to be found. On the wall above the row of counters is a large, yellow banner saying, in large lettering, *'PRIORITISE SELF SERVICE: QUICK, EASY, AND CHEAP. DON'T BE SWAYED BY BROKERS' OFFERS'*. On the furthest wall of counters, an announcement has been taped up detailing the government's official fee, written in letters and numbers that could not be clearer: two hundred and seventy thousand rupiah.

The clock hands are slowly crawling to the number ten, and people seem to keep coming from the main doorway. Of course, this waiting room is packed, with people coming in non-stop. Are there that many citizens of this country who can afford to go overseas?

'Ma'am, you were born out of wedlock, weren't you?' Bloody hell! The man named Oleng is suddenly at my side, throwing outrageous questions at me.

I immediately stare at this person, eyes widened, and ask: 'What do you mean?'

'Gosh, I'm sorry, Ma'am, here's the deal…'

I feel truly insulted.

'Here's the deal, Ma'am. Don't get upset already. This is so we're both comfortable, and everything goes smoothly. Ends quickly.'

'Hey! I'm a legitimate child. My mother was holding a bouquet when she entered the house. You understand what I mean? My mother was officially wed in front of guests and family.'

'I believe you. Of course I believe you. But here's the deal, Ma'am, what I mean is: you can't prove this by bringing your parents' marriage certificate, can you, Ma'am? Right? That could make things complicated, Ma'am. Could be complicated. So that's why I said you were born out of wedlock. So when they ask you later, just say you are. If not, they're going to ask for your father's papers, your mother's complete papers, all kinds of this and that. The point is, it'll be complicated. Trust me.'

The noisy waiting room suddenly feels quiet. The face of Mr Oleng with its moving mouth, then him pointing and pointing at me, 'Ma'am, you've been called. Go there immediately.'

I'm still not hearing him.

'Ma'am! You've been called!' Mr Oleng gives me a good smack on the shoulder. 'If they ask you, don't forget to say yes.'

Now I'm in a different room, this time with a young, dapper officer, with a clean face and narrowing eyes that look unblinkingly at my shorts. I'm standing there confused, and before deciding to quickly sit down, the young, dapper, narrow-eyed officer begins to speak. His voice is low.

'Ma'am, you need to change into long pants, then we can let you in. Otherwise, I'll gladly reject your passport application,' he motions me away with the back of his hand, expressionless. It feels quite cruel. The cold AC air, flowing from behind his stiff frame, blasting at me mercilessly.

'Would it be possible…'

'Please leave, Ma'am!'

Holy shit. This is some hardcore treatment. I'm outraged, at wit's end. Not daring to answer, I leave the room. And the young officer immediately calls the next number in line, paying me no attention. Outside, Mr Oleng hurries over and stares at me, confused.

'What's the matter?'

'You didn't tell me to begin with that I'm not allowed to wear shorts in a government office.'

'But the shorts you have are quite decent, aren't they, Ma'am? So what happened?'

'Why are you asking me? Now take me home to change into long pants. Or take me to the nearest clothing store.'

'Oh, my goodness. This doesn't usually happen, Ma'am. And it's impossible to leave. The office will close soon. You won't make it. Or how about this, let's swap pants.'

'What?'

'Swap pants, Ma'am. Hehe…' Mr Oleng is shaking his head. 'There's no other way, is there?'

No other way, he says. I shake my head and say, 'Not with your pants.'

I have to look around desperately for opportunities in girls with my body type. Going around worriedly, spinning my wheels and looking to and fro. Mr Oleng the Overlord, the office employee who is supposedly esteemed, begins to bumble:

'I apologise, Ma'am. Seems like that rule was just put in place today, somehow. The rules do usually change a lot. Gosh, and your shorts are quite chaste in my opinion, Ma'am.'

I act like a fool, popping up suddenly in front of a few women, moving slowly closer to them, then asking for something impossible and ridiculous.

'Could I borrow your pants for a bit? Let's swap for a little while. Just a little while. I'm not being allowed into the interview room, just because of these shorts.'

Nice-smelling women. Women with hair-polished hair. Women with expensive face powder. Women armpitting bags from famous brands. Women with diamond necklaces. Women with plenty of accessories. Young women. Older women. Every honourable and decent woman I approach desperately in the waiting room. Every one says no. Some are mean and give me nasty looks. One even shrieks, 'You're crazy!' So I come to my next outrageous idea, an even more desperate act: the toilets, the caretaker. So that's where I run to. I hope the officer in question is a woman.

'Miss, can I borrow your pants? Let's swap for a bit. I'll give you a tip for your kindness. Please, is that OK?' I say, as though I've found the last good woman on the planet.

The girl stares innocently at me. Finally, she answers, 'Yes,' without any further questions. Just as I'd suspected, those thought of as 'little people' have larger hearts. Both of us enter the toilets. The awful smell and disgusting floor bother me as I take my shorts off. The girl's taken her pants off. I'm half-naked too. We both stoop, embarrassed. Whatever the situation is, it's really uncomfortable for women to have to look at each other's underwear. Slowly, I put my feet through the girl's still-warm pants. What can I say. They only reach my thighs, and I can't pull them up any further.

My last hope rests with the ficus tree. The spot for other 'little people'. And below the ficus tree is a woman selling pecel lele, the fried catfish dish, wearing a sarong. Is a sarong cloth long enough to be acceptable? There's no time to think. I begin to feel resigned, and more accurately: to feel hopeless.

'Wanna eat, Miss?' she asks. I stand stock still in front of the woman. Her body size isn't so different from mine, and that sarong cloth is what I need.

'I'll eat later, if that's OK, Ms. I'm in need of pants or a long skirt, or even your sarong. As long as it's not shorts. I'm serious, Ms. Just to borrow to wear for a little while. No longer than an hour. Do you want to lend me your sarong?'

'Sure, Miss. But this sarong of mine's really dirty. Won't you be embarrassed?'

'It's OK, Ms. Better than nothing. The important thing is, it's long. That's the rule. I live far from here, and the immigration office is closing soon. Let's swap in the toilets.'

*

Now I feel relieved, and am sitting calmly in the waiting room. Mr Oleng has reentered the interview counter, speaking about this and that to the cruel young officer – whatever it is they're talking about, perhaps negotiating the sarong I'm wearing, or offering a new price, I don't want to think about it. The fan spinning above my head feels truly refreshing, having felt hot just a few moments ago, from walking to and fro anxiously. But over time, several people sitting to my left and right seem to be staring at me with disgusted faces.

'Kind of smells like shrimp paste, doesn't it?' a heavy woman says snidely in my direction, wealthy-seeming from her shiny, salon-coiffed wide bun. I don't care, of course. Shrimp paste smell? A bad, worn-out sarong? I know all that. I just didn't anticipate that the shrimp paste, which might have been on every part of the sarong I was wearing, would truly stink the place up so much.

'Yeah. It didn't stink before, did it? Suddenly it stinks now. Not the smell of shrimp paste, but the smell of rotting meat,' a white-haired Chinese woman says, rubbing her nose with her forefinger. She must have deliberately added the term 'rotting meat' to deride my presence more cuttingly.

'A rotten smell,' the woman sitting next to that Chinese woman says, standing immediately. *Well, go ahead, stand, all of you go,* I think, of course not caring one bit. To hell with it. Imagine the strange smell of shrimp paste suddenly spreading amongst nice-smelling fragrances, going wherever it likes with the help of the breeze from a fan. Of course, it's fabulous. And I smile, imagining a room cooled by the AC behind the cruel young officer.

'Madam Tjhang Chai Ha! Madam Thjang Chai Ha!'

I hurry to enter and answer to my name. Turns out the office employee Mr Oleng, who doesn't want to be called a hustler, still has some power after all. I'd been waiting for only five minutes, and my name is already being summoned.

I sit in front of the young officer from before. This time he starts sniffing.

'Smells like shrimp paste, doesn't it?'

His question makes the others in that AC-ed room sniff, and stop their interviews momentarily. Feeling tickled and not wanting to delay matters, I speak up.

'Here are the papers.'

The young officer is still busy following his nose, his narrowed eyes looking towards my sarong. The AC air quickly transfers that miraculous smell to all corners of the room. Mercilessly, of course. The nostrils of the young officer flare more and more. He looks me over again and again, from my face, to the sarong, back to the face. Confused, he hurries to ask me a quick series of questions: the name of my mother, my age, how many siblings, and where I'm going with the passport I'm requesting. And it's done.

Having left the immigration office, I feel relief. As quickly as possible, I walk towards the woman selling pecel lele, give her a tip, and slip my shorts back on as I thank her: 'Your sarong has brought blessings to this immigration office.'

The ficus tree growing in the yard of the immigration office begins, for whatever reason, to suddenly feel cooling. The breeze blowing against my chest feels ample, though it's high noon. Perhaps it's because I'm picturing the smell that will continue to settle there, though it's only the smell of shrimp paste. Who knows, perhaps the white-haired Chinese woman, who'd been sitting next to me on the bench, is now facing an officer? And perhaps she is saying decisively that the interview room doesn't smell like shrimp paste, but like rat carcasses. Who knows. What I do know is that I am now sitting comfortably in the car, laughing as Mr Oleng says: 'How come this car smells like shrimp paste?'

Notes

1. Lebaran: the holiday period at the end of Ramadan, around the time of Idul Fitri.
2. Ci: Miss, used in the Chinese-Indonesian community.

The Problem

Sabda Armandio

Translated by Rara Rizal

24 SEPTEMBER IS THE day Gembok brings his new friend along.

17:00

It is physically impossible for Yuli to get properly drunk, because as soon as enough liquor – or coffee, for that matter – goes in, something else will rise from the pit of her stomach. She will fight to keep everything down, of course, but eventually her body will take over, leaving her retching and surrendering in tears. And Yuli is especially sober at the moment, so when she sees Gembok arriving at her door, she does not expect to see this man standing beside him. He looks about Gembok's age, or perhaps a little younger, in a crisp buttoned shirt, dark grey trousers and a pair of loafers. Yuli has never seen the man before, but come to think of it, it isn't unlike Gembok to bring new people over. She has been friends with him long enough to know that he would be the last person to harbour suspicions towards anyone. After all, Gembok is the kind of person who always sees the glass as half full, the kind who believes that people are inherently good.

At least he's got conviction.

The line between naïve and foolish can be as thin as the first string on the guitar.

My strings are fine, thank you very much.

The stranger offers his hand to introduce himself. Seeing no other option, Yuli does what one is expected to be polite.

For fuck's sake, I don't have time for this right now. Let me go back to my nap.

Yuli wants nothing more than to get back to her nap, and right now she is not interested in small talk. She wishes that these men would leave her alone.

That goes for you, too.

And so Yuli will be left alone for now.

18:00

As soon as she wakes up, Yuli realises Gembok and his friend are still chatting outside. She can hear their mindless rambling from the other side of the room – something about rich people and their penchant for trouble. At one point their conversation turns personal. Gembok is talking about street life now, how different it is, how in this world a college degree is the last thing you need to survive.

For Yuli, it's time to get up.

Time to step outside, walk across the small alley to Bibi's warung, and get herself a cup of hot tea.

Can you maybe, for once, not tell me what to do?

Despite her protest, Yuli manages to drag herself to the warung and order a cup of hot tea. She accepts the complementary sweet buns from Bibi as a thank-you gift for taking the lady's son to school earlier that morning.

Jeez. I guess not.

It seems that Yuli is still not in the mood for socialising, but there is nowhere else to go. Her plastic cup in hand, she walks to the front porch and sits down to join the two men on the floor. She offers them the sweet buns as she reaches for the songbook. It was Yuli's idea. At first, Gembok thought it unnecessary, and not to mention a rookie thing to do – writing down song lyrics and chords – but it wasn't long before he saw the benefit of having a songbook: they would never run out of songs to play when they are out busking.

Sensing that the new friend seems to have taken a liking to Yuli, Gembok proceeds to tell him how he met Yuli for the first time. Yuli lets him talk. Gembok is honest to a fault, the kind of person that tells things as they are with no embellishments, so Yuli can always trust his version of the story and doesn't feel that she has to interrupt or correct him.

Besides, the new friend seems eager to share his story as well.

'I've been a fan of Fugazi since junior high,' he begins. Something clicks in Yuli's mind, and she is beginning to figure out why Gembok likes this person enough to bring him here. The new friend seems to warm up to them fairly quickly –

Far too quickly.

– and before long, he is confiding in them about how life was rough for him as a child, especially after his parents got divorced. Oh, and speaking of parents, where to start. His father would always tell him to grab the bull by its horn, do something worthwhile with his life. 'That's rich coming from someone who couldn't tame his own demons. He was a drunk, and he would spend all his money on gambling. Sometimes he would hit me, and things would get really nasty, but once he sobered up, he would apologise and blame it on the alcohol. It was absurd. When my mother finally told him she wanted a divorce, he begged for her pity. He said it was his father's fault, because *his* father used to beat *him* up, too. And that's ironic, because –'

A mongrel walks by and stops by Yuli's side.

Gembok pats his new friend on the shoulder, and asks if he would like to help them get the guitar and mini drums ready since it's almost time to hit the road. Yuli just sits there, scratching the mongrel's head.

'You coming with us?' asks Gembok.

The new friend shakes his head. 'I've got someplace to be. Perhaps tomorrow.'

19:00

They know these streets by heart: the deafening noise of engines, the endless honking, and the occasional shouting and cursing you'd would expect from grumpy drivers during peak hours. What they do not expect, however, is a motorcycle weaving through the intersection just as the light turns red, almost knocking over Gembok who is busy tapping on his mini drums. Gembok stands frozen, still reeling from the shock, but Yuli will not have it. She puts down her guitar, leaps to the motorcycle to grab the key from the ignition, and throws it to the sidewalk. The motorist is furious and is yelling at her now, but Yuli is unfazed. She shrugs, then points at the red light. She picks up her guitar and continues playing.

We are all desperate to get home, some more than others. It's understandable. People get impatient when they're exhausted.

Boohoo. We're all exhausted. It's not an excuse to be a dick.

Later, during their break, Gembok slowly regains his composure. 'He was just lashing out,' he says. 'It happens, you know. People lash out all the time. It makes them feel better.'

Yuli does not completely disagree. 'I wonder what it is that they're going through to think that it's OK to run people over in the middle of the street like that.'

'Some kind of trouble at work, maybe. Who knows.'

The Palmerah junction has been their busking spot for the past two years now. Staying alert is part of the job because, at any time, Satpol PP[1] can come and raid the area, looking to catch illegal street vendors or round up prostitutes and buskers. If they spot the khaki uniform from afar, Yuli and Gembok will pack up their things and get going, hiding somewhere until the raid is over.

But this time is different. Instead of Satpol PP, a whole platoon of police officers are now roaming the streets. Police presence usually means something more serious is going on. Yuli and Gembok know better than to stick around, so the two quickly dash to Bibi's warung.

When they arrive, Bibi is watching the news. The riots have spread across the country. In Jakarta, protests outside the parliament building have turned violent. Police are combing through streets and residential areas, chasing and arresting people.

'Those bastards.'

One should refrain from making such comments. Lashing out is rarely useful in situations like this.

I didn't ask for your advice. Let me just lash out, OK? That's what's useful to me right now, and not some unsolicited –

Suddenly, a loud crash. Yuli turns her head to look for the source, and from the end of the alley she sees a figure stumbling towards her. It appears that the person has tripped and knocked over a trash can. He gets back on his feet, and Yuli recognises him. It's Gembok's new friend.

Gembok rushes to his side, grabs him by the arms, and slowly guides him to a chair beside Yuli.

'Fucking pigs,' he says, taking a seat. His eyes are red, and he reeks of sweat and pepper. He hasn't fully caught his breath when he starts to rant. 'A bunch of lazy, incompetent crooks, those lawmakers, every single one of them! And yet, when it comes to a bill that would benefit the elites, all of a sudden they're working round the clock trying to get it out as quickly as possible. They are going to jeopardise *everything* that the Reformasi[2] has achieved in the last two decades! Did they really think they could get away with it? Is it any wonder that the people are angry?' He pauses for a moment.

'All we wanted to do was protest, yet they chased us down like *we* were the thugs.'

Yuli cannot help but feel for him. White collars don't normally pay attention to politics *du jour*, let alone care about complicated affairs such as the democratic process. Perhaps, he is a Fugazi fan after all.

Stop being a smartass.

He resents his father, he's frustrated with his job and the petty office politics, so he finds the perfect target to channel all that rage: the government.

I don't think it's that deep.

Yuli doesn't completely disagree.

See, again with the assumptions.

It's a deduction rather than an assumption.

'You know what's crazy? Not a single person at work was interested in joining the protest,' he says, 'Even though this affects them, too. I swear, these people. Just a bunch of fish in a bowl.'

Yuli asks Bibi to make another cup of tea for him, while Gembok pats him on the back, trying to get him to calm down. But as soon as he sips his tea, he picks up right where he left off, cursing at the police before shifting his outrage to his mates at the office. But naturally, the most colourful profanities are reserved for the boss, because who else would force their employees to work overtime with no pay unless they're a psychopath. And honestly, he swears to God, this job is a deal with the devil, the boss being the Devil himself.

'You sell your soul, and for what? Once you're in it, there's no way out. *Industry 4.0* – what a load of crap.'

He starts sobbing. Gembok extends his arm to embrace him, trying to think of things to say.

23:00

The light turns red. Yuli steps into the middle of the road, Gembok and his mini drums trailing behind her. It's showtime. The car in front of them, a red jeep, flashes its headlight. Yuli squints, but she keeps singing. Suddenly, the jeep jumps forward. Gembok is gesturing at Yuli to get out of the way, and she does, just as the car speeds through the red light.

'I think that guy was a cop,' says Yuli.

'Everyone's a cop to you.' Gembok chuckles.

'Remember the bakso peddler I suspected was undercover? Guess what, turns out he really was.'

'Yeah? And what about the other hawkers you also suspected were cops?'

'Think about it. Have you seen the news lately? For all I know your new friend could be a cop.'

'OK, suppose the guy just now really was an undercover cop. Why did you insist on blocking his way?'

'Because he's a cop!'

They finish counting their earnings for the day. They always divide the money equally between them, but not before sparing a small portion of the earnings for what Yuli calls the cash reserve. Gembok did not fully understand why they needed to do that, until one day a cab ran over his foot, and Yuli used it to pay for his treatment. Gembok hasn't complained about it since then.

29 September is the day we discover that Gembok's new friend is too emo to be a cop.

19:25

Yuli and Gembok are playing the third song on their setlist when suddenly a group of protesters from the Senayan stadium are running in their direction. Someone from the crowd is shouting their names. It's Gembok's new friend. 'The cops are everywhere,' he says. 'Let's get out of here.'

The three of them find shelter at Bibi's warung.

'I used to be in a punk band,' says Gembok's new friend. 'We played The Sex Pistols, mostly.'

The Sex Pistols is not even punk, at least not according to Yuli, who thinks that the anti-establishment attitude was all just an act, because let's face it, a lot of people use punk as an excuse to – in her own words – be a dick.

Perhaps Yuli should say something about it, then.

Look, I'm not in the mood to have a pointless debate with someone who thinks he knows everything just because he 'used to be in a band'.

But this is a subject that Yuli and Gembok are quite knowledgeable about. The new friend is still going on and on about The Sex Pistols, yet he has not said anything about Nancy Spungen or how she was vilified by the media in a twisted attempt by music journalists to sell their tabloids. Instead, Gembok's new friend keeps bringing up outdated but pointless band trivia as if he was the first person they heard it from. Clearly, he needs to be humbled. Yuli is ready to jump in any time now.

You do know I don't always have to have a take on everything?

One should always speak up about the things one knows. This is how one gains the respect of others.

Right. As if talking about The Sex Pistols will all of a sudden make him respect me. If anything –

At least that way he'll know that Yuli is not as clueless as he thinks.

I don't need to prove myself to him. But fine. You want me to say something, I'll say something.

Yuli shifts in her seat, and begins. 'You want to know what I think? There's nothing punk about getting high and drunk and acting out all the time. If they were really fighting for freedom, which I doubt they were, then their idea of freedom was breaking curfew to party all night. Perfect role models for teenagers.'

'You see, we don't do parties,' says Gembok, trying to lighten up the conversation. 'And maybe that's why we don't necessarily relate.'

21.47

The three of them are walking along Palmerah Street, chatting aimlessly while scanning the area to look for a safe spot to set up their instruments. This is the most fun Gembok's new friend has had in a long time, he confesses. Aside from the co-workers at his boring job, there's no one to talk to, no one to engage in intense and passionate conversations with, not even about *ordinary* topics like which operating system is better: MacOS or Windows, iPhone or Android, you know, that sort of stuff. Gembok and Yuli just stare at each other.

'I used to think I was different to most people,' he says, 'You know, I'm *wired* different. I tend to choose the path not taken. But then one day I realised that I'm just a cog in the machine. There's nothing special about doing the same things over and over again, stuck in a loop, in service of –'

It is then that Yuli finally realises for sure that Gembok's new friend is too emo to be a cop.

Alright, listen. I never seriously thought he was a cop.

Despite her denial, Yuli actually did at one point suspect Gembok's new friend of being some sort of secret cop, or at least he wished he was one, or perhaps that he was related to someone who was. But that was before she heard him saying 'I'm just a cog in the machine.' And then, come to think of it, there is all that business about his father.

Nah. I think he's just emo.

Now Yuli begins to think that perhaps Gembok's new friend was, after all, just emo.

'Strange world we live in,' says Gembok's new friend. 'You've been a rebel all your life. And then one day you wake up and you're sucked into it all. It's quicksand. I mean it literally. It sucks you dry. It's like, picture this for a moment: imagine you're in a line trying to get into a Slipknot concert.'

'I can't imagine ever wanting to go to a Slipknot concert,' cuts Yuli.

'Alright, then, what about this. You're trying to eat at your favourite warung, the best one in town. It's so good, so popular, right, that people are lining up in a queue waiting to get in. But lucky for you, you have enough money to pay people to queue for you. Do you see what's wrong here? Has anyone ever stopped to think about how everything we do revolves around money? I mean, who decided that we needed money in the first place? And who benefits from having money? I think about this all the time.'

Gembok nods. The analogy seems to make sense at first, until Yuli realises that no warung is actually ever that crowded to begin with. Educated people sometimes make things up just to prove a point.

Actually, it wasn't that bad an analogy.

Actually, she is right. It wasn't that bad.

23:00

A familiar car stops at the intersection. The red jeep has been showing up on their busking spot every day for the past few days now, and always around the same time. Sometimes it speeds right by, but if the light happens to be red, it will slow down and stop just as Gembok and Yuli start singing. The driver never gives them any money. Yuli thinks there is something suspicious about the car.

'I tried to peek through the window, but all I could see

was the tape player on the dashboard,' says Yuli during their break. She leans into the rolling door of a closed shop.

'Well, it's really hard to look inside when the window is tinted,' says Gembok's new friend.

Yeah, no shit.

'What did you think you were going to find, anyway?' says Gembok, playing with his drumsticks. 'Even if he's a cop, so what? We have no business snooping around.'

'Or maybe he's a reporter,' says Gembok's new friend, 'You know, covering the protest. An investigative journalist, or a photographer, or something.'

'I doubt it,' says Yuli. 'Those people don't normally go around with a car. Motorcycles are more practical. Easier to manoeuvre through traffic.'

'For all we know, he could just be someone from around here,' says Gembok. 'I mean, look at his jeep. The red stands out too much. Cops usually prefer black, or camo.'

'She has a point, though,' says Gembok's new friend. 'Things have been out of control lately. Have you heard about the cop who drove a barracuda straight through the crowd? They even shot people dead.'

'This reminds me,' says Gembok, 'I'm thinking of joining the protest.'

'Then come with me tomorrow. We'll go together.'

30 September is the day Yuli, Gembok, and his new friend join the protest.

22:15

They are too exhausted to sleep and too restless to stay in, so they decide to head out again.

Yuli cannot stop replaying the images in her head from earlier that day. There is something so surreal about it all: the streets and landmarks look so familiar from where she stands, but everything else isn't, because she is trapped in the crowd and she is surrounded by cops, who keep shooting tear gas and firecrackers. Yuli has always felt like she belonged in these streets, and yet for the first time ever, she wishes she could get out of there, if only so she could breathe. Inhaling tear gas is like breathing in millions of tiny shards that travel through your nose, your eyes, all the way down your lungs, and your body –

That's not what I think.

That may not be exactly what Yuli is thinking, but it was what she was experiencing at that moment.

You know absolutely nothing about what I went through back there. Leave me alone. Please.

Yuli starts sobbing.

She is left alone for now.

23:00

They arrive at the Palmerah junction. A man lies on the sidewalk, unconscious. Beside him, someone is screaming for help. The three run across the street to get to him. 'We were beaten up by the cops. I'm fine, I think, but he's... I can't leave him here,' he says. 'They're still sweeping this entire block, and I'm afraid they're going to come back.'

Suddenly, a familiar car approaches. Gembok chases the jeep until it finally slows down and backs up. Gembok approaches the driver, and after a moment he runs back and gestures at the man lying on the ground.

'Help me lift him.'

This is all too much. Yuli wants to stop them, but she hesitates. She settles on asking Gembok if he knows where to go.

'The General Hospital, behind Atmajaya,' says Gembok. 'You two stay here, I'll take them. They came all the way from

Bandung to join the protest, so they're going to need help with directions.'

Gembok hops onto the jeep, leaving Yuli alone with his new friend. The two watch as the car slowly disappears from view.

3 October and Gembok has not returned to Bibi's warung.

Bibi is busy tapping on her calculator, counting the bill for a customer while saying each item out loud. Two iced tea. One rice. One tempe. Four sweet buns. Twenty-two thousand. Behind her, a government spokesperson on TV is reading names of people off of a list: dead, injured, whereabouts unknown, arrested for disorderly conduct.

Disorderly. I hate that word. What did they expect? For people to show up to the protest, take out a mat, and have a picnic? It's been three days since I last saw Gembok, and for the past three days I've been watching the news, hoping to see his name on the list.

'Look at them speak. Like fish in a bowl,' I say to Gembok's new friend, who has been sitting beside me, eyes glued to the TV. He turns to me.

'Oh hey, I said that!' He chuckles. 'Oh well, I also heard it from someone else.'

'Have you heard from Gembok?'

He shakes his head.

'Do you think maybe we should start looking for him?' I ask.

'What? Where? How?'

I really don't have the patience right now for someone who answers a question with more questions, so I just stare at him.

'What I mean is,' he says, 'We filed a report, and the officer told us they'll be in touch. We've done everything we could by the book.'

'Maybe that's the problem,' I say, almost to myself. I turn to him. 'Listen. Do you want to help?'

Gembok's new friend takes a long look at me, and nods. I offer my hand for a real introduction this time. 'Good. But first, what was your name again?'

Notes

1. Satuan Polisi Pamong Praja (or Satpol PP): the municipal police units in Indonesia which are under local government control, overseen by the Ministry of Affairs.

2. Reformasi: the period after the resignation of authoritarian president Suharto in 1998.

Buyan[1]

utiuts

Translated by Zoë McLaughlin

AUNTIE NANA'S DRIVERLESS CAR was stupid. Maybe the car hadn't read the news that half of Jakarta was underwater. The government was seeking to conduct an emergency reclamation, but the problem was that their headquarters were also submerged. Where could they have their coordination meetings? It had now been almost a year since they'd closed off half of Jakarta.

Because she was too busy editing selfies on SnapGram, Auntie Nana stopped paying attention to the route. The car rolled leisurely down the usual streets – she thought she would reach her relatives' house in Cipete in no time. Ultimately, it was the horn's incessant honking that forced Auntie Nana to look up from her favourite social media app. She was confused. Patung Dirgantara was on her right, and instead of turning left to Pancoran, the driverless car had continued straight. It seemed to be heading towards Semanggi. Auntie Nana panicked and called her niece.

'Denis, help! My car is heading to Central Jakarta. How do I stop it? There's no driver.'

'Open the app, Auntie. If you click menu, it should link to the help centre. Contact them,' answered Denis.

'Can you not call them? Tell them I'm going to drown!'

'How am I supposed to do that, Auntie? When you called

the car, you used the app, didn't you? Why didn't you just take a normal taxi?'

'Oh honestly, Denis, it was pouring at Halim airport earlier. The queue for the taxis was so long it reached the next terminal. I called a Kejar and the only one that answered was this stupid car.'

'Why didn't you pick one with a driver? You can do that in the app. Driverless cars are still being tested.'

'Ugh, I don't know! In Palembang, all the Kejars have drivers. Where's that menu in the app? Stop distracting me with your nonsense. I'm already at Gatot Subroto!'

Ever since the city had been paralysed by floods, the dry neighbourhoods in East and South Jakarta had seen rapid development. Unfortunately, that growth was not quite in step with the growth of access lanes or overpasses to reach them. In fact, some areas were still more quickly accessed via the Inner Ring Road. It was towards this loop that Auntie Nana's 'sophisticated' car was now taking her. With the assistance of Denis, she found the help centre in the app.

'How am I supposed to call them? I can't read English.'

'There's a telephone symbol, Auntie.'

She found the symbol Denis meant and pressed it, hanging up on her at the same time. A computer operator answered Auntie Nana's call.

'Press one for service in Indonesian.' Then in English, *'Press two —'*

Auntie Nana screamed in frustration and jabbed at the number one on her screen with the tip of her nail. Didn't the Kejar people know she was in a hurry? How many numbers did she have to push just to talk to customer service?

'To ensure the services we provide remain the best, your conversation with the operator will be recorded,' said the computer operator. After a few tense moments, the voice of a human operator finally took over.

'Good afternoon, you've reached Kejar. How can we help you?'

'Please help – my car is driving itself to Semanggi. Please stop it.'

'With whom am I speaking? Can you give me your customer number, Ma'am?'

'Listen, you idiot. This is an *emergency*! Just look on your computer for the car that's headed to Semanggi. Quickly, Dik!2 I'll be underwater soon!'

The operator asked her to wait and Auntie Nana was forced to listen to Avi Rahmat in the new Kejar advert. Auntie Nana saw and heard Avi Rahmat everywhere – on the radio, the TV, and now even on the telephone. How much money was Avi Rahmat making! He seemed in high demand. What if just appearing on info-tainment made him money?

'Ma'am, thank you for waiting. We are currently looking into the issue. It seems there's been an error in the taxi's mapping system – I'm afraid your car is still using an old map of Jakarta. We apologise for the inconvenience.'

'It's easy for you to apologise... now get to how to stop it!'

'We're currently updating your car's mapping system and taking control of the steering from here. You don't need to worry. Please hold –'

'Hello? Hello?'

Avi Rahmat returned, replacing the live operator, who had vanished. The celebrity's high-pitched voice continued promoting Kejar. 'Kejar is offering a fifty per cent discount with Driverless Kejars! Nana, because you've already ridden Driverless Kejar, your next trip will be free!'

Avi Rahmat was getting rather familiar with Auntie Nana. These hyper-targeted ads were designed to turn consumers into friends, but this time Kejar was unsuccessful. Auntie Nana felt she was being manipulated. Her ears buzzed, breaking her concentration. She saw she had reached

Balai Kartini. The dashboard showed that the car was still moving consistently at 40 kilometres per hour, taking her closer and closer to Semanggi. Auntie Nana could see the barrier and waterline at the end of the road. Even though the car's air conditioning was blasting cool air, sweat marks appeared on the underarms of her shirt.

'Hello? Have you talked to them?' shouted Auntie Nana at her smartphone. As if hearing Auntie Nana's shouts, the operator returned once again.

'Ma'am, we're very sorry. We haven't yet succeeded in taking control of your car because of –' then in English, '– an interrupted connection.'

'What does that mean? Just speak Indonesian.'

'Interrupted connection,' repeated the operator, in English.

'In Indonesian! Please, Dik, I'm drowning!'

'There's no signal, Ma'am, we –'

'What? How are you this stupid! You can make this car drive itself, but you can't get a signal? Where's your boss? I want to talk to them!' screamed Auntie Nana.

'We apologise, Ma'am, we can't –'

'It's been "we can't" from the very beginning. This conversation is being recorded, right? Then record *this*, send it to your supervisors! Instead of paying Avi Rahmat so much, better to use the money to find a signal or to pay for drivers. I don't care how you do it, just stop this car now! If I die, I'll haunt you and seven generations of your descendants. If I live, I'll complain about you on SnapGram. I have three thousand followers, you know.'

'Ma'am, please remain calm, we are sending a rescue team. Please stay on the line.'

'Rescue, my arse! The water is right in front of me. How do you stop this thing! Help, I'm about to die!'

Auntie Nana's stupid car crashed into the wooden barrier that separated the dry road from the wet one. Auntie Nana screamed in fear, interspersed with prayers, pleading with the car to stop at once. But the car had no ears. The operator was the one listening. 'Oh God, oh God, oh God,' said the operator.

'Where's the rescue team? There's water coming into the car. Help me! I came to Jakarta to visit my husband's grave, not to follow him,' sobbed Auntie Nana.

The water seeping into the car was already dampening her ankles. Auntie Nana lifted her feet and curled up in the passenger seat, howling miserably at the operator. The Samsat Building looked down on the car in front of it, parked and immobile. It turned out Auntie Nana's car had stopped moving. *What?*

Auntie Nana stopped crying and looked around her, confused.

'Ma'am, Ma'am. Are you all right?' called the operator in a concerned voice, resembling that of her girlfriends when they asked why Auntie Nana hadn't remarried.

Auntie Nana read the warning on the car's dashboard screen.

'It says, "Warning! Chharjs your kar to kontinyu your terip." What does that mean?'

'Alhamdulillah, ya rabbi, your car's battery has run out, so it stopped. You can get out now – the central lock can be unlocked manually.'

'So you expect me to swim, do you? Come get me now! Use a boat or a helicopter, whatever you like.'

Auntie Nana hung up and picked up tissue after tissue. She wiped her tears and her wet feet. Once she reached the house, she would have each and every one of her relatives delete this stupid app. If necessary, Denis could help them all delete it. Her siblings were all stupid.

Using the camera on her smartphone, Auntie Nana made sure her makeup was still in place. Then she opened SnapGram and recorded a video.

Notes

1. Buyan: a word meaning 'stupid' in the Palembang language. Palembang is one of over 700 languages spoken across Indonesia. It is used here to demonstrate the linguistic diversity of the capital city.

2. Dik (short for Adik): a word meaning a younger sibling or someone younger than you in general.

A Secret from Kramat Tunggak

Dewi Kharisma Michellia

Translated by Shaffira Gayatri

SHE ENTERED THE APARTMENT and closed the door behind her. She was even more exhausted than usual tonight, but upon seeing the spilt beer and bottles scattered on the floor, coupled with a few dozen cigarette butts filling the ashtray on the table, she suddenly felt like breaking something.

As she slammed the door, a few disturbing noises escaped from the next room: the rusty pegs of the old mattress, one moan upon another, one thrust upon another. This, despite reminding her mother hundreds of times to stop doing sex work in their home.

Six months ago, her mother had broken the bad news at their regular lapo,[1] while she was busy munching on her favourite Karo-style grilled pork.

'Help me out,' her mother begged at the time. 'We need to settle our debts to those loan sharks,' she said, before explaining her decision to return to her old profession, all the while hungrily chomping on the grilled pork.

Sensing that permission from her was unnecessary, she ended the discussion. 'Take care of your own business, then. Your debt is not my responsibility.'

Her mother's cry of God's name from the next bedroom, followed by a piercing shriek, broke her reverie. Her mother and her punter, God knows who, continued to wrestle wildly, just like any other night. 'This mother of yours was once the prima donna of Kramat Tunggak,' she had announced proudly, while they were getting up to leave the lapo. 'We could make a lot of money.'

She frowned. For one, she could provide for herself. After all, wasn't she the one paying their rent? *Make a lot of money?* She didn't need more!

But her pride prevented her from demanding an explanation of how her mother racked up such debts. Of the pair of them, she was the one who worked harder. And what she was sure of was that she wanted a clean break with Kramat Tunggak. Although her childhood memories faded as each day passed, she knew that being there hadn't been the best of times for her and her mother.

As she grew older, she eventually discovered that Kramat Tunggak, or 'Kramtung' as the locals often call it, was the spell behind Jakarta's magic. With the taxes earned from the infamous red-light district, the governor was able to fund Jakarta's development, from city toll roads to the Taman Ismail Marzuki art and cultural complex.

Sounds cool, but for her, all that superficial justification meant nothing.

'I'm still pretty enough and wouldn't need to work much. Three guests a day would be enough to cover our debts and give us something to live on,' her mother went on.

'But Kramtung is our *past*,' she retorted.

'I didn't say we were going back!' her mother snapped.

So, here they were, in a rented apartment in Kalibata. Despite her attempt to show reluctance, like usual, she eventually gave in to her mother's decision. To help cover the first month's rent, she had to say goodbye to the money she'd put aside for her university fees that semester. And it was with silent curses and endless prejudices that she followed her mother's move to Kalibata.

Ever the sharp tongue, she called the place the 'Playground of Philanderers'.

It was a cramped, noisy residential complex with all kinds of human beings imaginable: from office workers, traders, and students, to drug dealers and hookers. They called it an apartment development, a dignified title, complete with a shopping mall, basketball courts, and scores of cafés. But it was also a haven for kerb-crawlers, a headquarters for pot dealers, and a place where a heartbroken girl jumped from the eighth floor. In short, it was a cursed hell-hole.

All this would come in handy as ammunition any time she needed to angrily vent at her mother: 'Why did we have to move to this damned place?!'

On the morning they moved in to their new place, she bumped into a man her age, fully naked, banging on the door of the unit next to them. Looking tipsy, the naked man gave them a welcoming smile, 'Whoa, hey there, new neighbours. Sorry, I lost a bet and those crazies inside tricked me into this.' Clutching an old cardboard box to cover his crotch, he continued to bang on the door.

The unit next door was occupied by five builders who worked for the contractor living in the unit next to theirs. They would leave early in the morning, and return late at night, their bodies damp with sweat and their clothes filthy. Plumes of smoke engulfed the hallway as they hung out after work.

Ironically, with those kind of neighbours she quickly felt at home. She made friends with the naked man, his builder friends, and the contractor, often sharing cigarettes or lending each other lighters. One time one of them offered her Valium, which she politely declined.

Her mother swiftly picked up on her networking. Despite no longer being young, the number of 'clients' that need her service kept growing, from sleazy middle-aged men to pubescent high schoolers. Her mother was, admittedly, still ravishing. Even so, she knew quite well that her mother would need makeup, new clothes, and sexy lingerie that would arouse the carnal lust of even the most pious of men. In other words, her mother would need some money from her to get started.

Her mother had aimed to serve three men a day to ensure a comfortable income, yet this was not always possible since her clients came whenever they felt like it. As it was a last-minute attempt to cover their debts which she had never fully agreed upon, she had to resign herself to the fact that all their earnings went straight into her mother's bank account. She was left to bear the brunt of it all: the moans, the shrieks, the thumping sounds of things falling, and the post-coital cleaning up.

This time, though, she didn't bother to help out with the cleaning, too tired to start their whole ritual of fighting again.

Her mother's last client of the day left at two in the morning. She heard her mother calling out to her, knowing she was still awake, typing away on her laptop.

'I bought you food, some nasi padang. Why is it still left untouched? It'll go to waste if you don't eat.'

As she gingerly started eating her nasi padang, her mother, looking fresh even after three clients, took out the trash.

The entire apartment was spotless, as if untouched by cigarette smoke or beer stains. Still, it smelt musty, the walls all mouldy and damp.

Her plate was soon empty, but her mother had yet to return. Knowing her habit of enjoying the small hours of the morning by going for walks and taking different routes each time, she turned on the TV and chose a movie to watch while she waited.

The quality of the pirated DVD was crap. She made a mental note to teach her mother to download pirated movies instead so that they would be spared this torture.

After graduating from high school, she almost didn't go to college. It was her mother's dream to send her daughter to university, but money was the problem. With her mother's reluctant permission, she took a job as a sales girl at a shopping mall. In two years, after researching all the cheaper private colleges and calculating her savings from work, she finally plucked up the courage to enrol herself.

She chose accounting, thinking that after graduating she could get a job in no time. At first she considered a Fine Arts major, thinking it suited her better, but her mother dismissed this at once, saying matter-of-factly, 'That degree is just for rich kids who don't need to work for money.'

While her mother took on a few jobs here and there – doing the laundry for three of their neighbours and selling some home-cooked food at the university canteen – she continued to work part-time at a café in Cikini, near their neighbourhood. From there, she earned enough to cover their bills and the university fees.

With just the two of them and no extravagant expenses, it baffled her how her mother had got into a situation where a loan shark was after them. Didn't she cover her own university fees? Not only did she work part-time at the café, she also earned some money from doing transcribing jobs for a lecturer from another faculty. But she had too big an ego to have her mother think that it bothered her, so decided to stop asking questions.

She knew full well that they were poor. Throughout her childhood, they had had to move from one shabby alleyway to another, from one riverbank to another. She had probably made friends with every young thug in Jakarta. To this day, she had never in all seriousness asked why they were so poor, or where her father was, or how her mother came to whore at Kramat Tunggak.

★

Her mother finally returned at four in the morning, carrying a bag of groceries from the market; some ingredients to make lodeh – a vegetable soup with coconut milk – and a whole chicken cut into pieces of four.

'We're having another feast again, aren't we?' she observed while helping her mother take out the groceries and wash the vegetables clean.

'The last client gave me a hundred thousand rupiah bonus before he left,' her mother answered, blushing. 'He works at a hotel, on the morning shift. Left in a rush so he could see his wife before work.'

'Before I came home last night I bought you another dozen pack of condoms and put them in the drawer. Pay me back later only when I need the money. Are you going for your check up at the health centre?'

In the last few weeks, her mother had been complaining of constant vaginal discharge, and they were worried she might have a cyst or even syphilis.

As she didn't work for a pimp, her mother knew she needed to be independent. A habit she'd taken from her Kramat Tunggak days was keeping a journal of her clients with short profiles, including how long they last in bed, how many position changes, whether they refuse to wear condoms, whether they insist on coming in her mouth or on performing bukkake. The journal also noted her ovulating days and her regular check-up results at the health centre, and most importantly, special notes if something felt off.

'I was quite energetic today, I don't think it's syphilis.'

Her daughter snorted. 'Energetic? That was beyond energetic, you were shrieking like a banshee! I was almost tempted to tell you off.'

Her mother laughed loudly. She was beaming, her face

decorated with visible beads of perspiration. Yet it was just last week that her mother shivered beneath the blanket and she had to take time off work to change the wet washcloth on her mother's forehead every few hours.

It reminded her of how, during the fever, her mother was delirious and kept mentioning Kramat Tunggak. She thought that going back to her old profession was making her mother relive past memories. Many times she even called her daughter the wrong name.

'You kept mentioning Kramtung and saying someone's name.'

She was raised with very little information about her mother's past, not that she cared much. But this time she wanted to hear the real story.

'So, how did you come to work there? And why did you stop?'

As far as she knew, most women would usually 'retire' from Kramat Tunggak when they turned 35. But she was born when her mother was 26 years old, and she did not remember being the child of a 'prima donna'. They lived in Kramat Tunggak until she was six years old. At the time, her mother worked as a local cleaner, or so she thought. It wasn't until she was older that she realised her mother was rather one of Kramat Tunggak's sex workers, or how notorious the neighbourhood of her childhood was.

Generous cuts of choko, aubergine, tomatoes, long beans, belinjo, dried shrimp, and baby corn were added into the pan. Her mother then started to work on the chicken parts that were being marinated in a bowl. At six, the breakfast meal was ready on the table, complete with warm rice. Her mother's promise to tell her the story prompted her to sit eagerly at the table, scooping the freshly-made lodeh soup and rice onto her plate.

Unexpectedly, her mother opened her story with a

confession: they were never on the run from loan sharks. The money her mother had been collecting for the last six months wasn't to cover her debts, but to realise her mother's plan: to migrate and work as domestic workers abroad. For this, they would need a substantial amount of money to pay the fees required by the recruitment agency.

'But I'll be graduating soon! We'll get better opportunities. I'll be working at a bank, earning tens of millions a month. Why would we need to look for work abroad?'

'We'll get more money as migrant workers,' her mother responded.

'Yes, and we'll face more risks too. Did you not watch the news about hundreds of migrant workers coming home in coffins? So many die from abuse, so many are raped.'

'Look, you don't need to work as a domestic worker. I'll do it. You can carry on your studies there, or find work with your degree. We can take care of each other that way.'

'If you want a lot of money, just keep on whoring and once I graduate, I'll work at a bank. Sounds good, OK?'

'We're migrating.'

'No!'

Her mother finally gave in. 'It's your father,' she said.

'He knows where we are. He's insane and is capable of anything. I don't mean to scare you, but I'm sure he wants to kill us.'

Her father, the man that she never met all her life.

She had asked about him a handful of times before, and her mother always had different stories every time. One time she said that he worked as a contractor out of town; another that he left her to marry another woman. The last time she mentioned him it was to say that he died after being hit by a truck. And now her mother had just resurrected him. Did she think he was Jesus?

'I don't feel that we need to run away from a coward like

him,' she responded, picking up her spoon. 'If it's true that he's still alive, he doesn't have a reason to suddenly show up after disappearing for twenty-two years! And to kill us? You gotta be kidding me.'

'He's getting out of prison this month.'

★

Kramat Tunggak, 1988, was the first indication that her father was capable of anything.

The lights were out. The deafening dangdut music that had been blasting since afternoon was replaced with the sound of raindrops falling on the rooftop. A man appeared in the front terrace of a brothel. Taking off his distro cap, he entered the living room and charged straight to the pimp's desk.

'Bastard! How dare you hide the goods from me!'

He had just heard from his friends, who were also the pimp's clients, of a prima donna in Kramat Tunggak, fresh from a small village in Indramayu. Her parents had been scammed and went bankrupt, and with faces full of tears were forced to give her away. While most sex workers hailing from other West Javanese towns such as Kuningan, Cimahi, or Sukabumi were widowed or middle-aged divorcees, this new diva was just eighteen and was still a virgin. The man's friend was the first client and he had paid a hefty price for the new girl's virginity. 'Still a virgin and her moves are out of this world! You'd better hurry before all the other guys get their dicks in first!'

The pimp, a chubby man with small eyes, faced the man with a bitter smile, 'You should've kept coming by more often! Now that you're a boss, you got yourself a mistress, hey? Didn't they say you're one of the army guys? Should've got one of those actress types ages ago, man!'

The brothels in this area were far-removed from the motels or luxurious hotels that high-end hookers enjoyed. Still, the house where her mother worked was the biggest there was, with twenty tables and a hundred chairs in the waiting room, a dancefloor with never-ending dangdut music playing beneath flashy disco lights, as well as a bar offering all kinds of beers and sodas. Sometimes people would just lounge about enjoying their beers. After all, it was cheaper than bars or nightclubs.

The damp bedrooms were small and narrow, complete with metal beds and filthy curtains. A mirror hung in each dirty, foul-smelling bathroom, with damp towels strewn about, unwashed despite having been used by endless horny men. The pungent smell of piss, spilt beer, and cigarette smoke emanated from most rooms.

Every now and then one of the girls' lovers would get blind drunk and go on a rampage. Fuelled by jealousy, they would even kill, despite the ban on knives and guns in the brothel.

Just a few days into her new job, her mother had seen a man being stabbed with a dagger, his body doubling over in pain, his intestines spilling out of his torn gut. The situation worsened as security guards released warning shots and ambulance sirens wailed in the background.

'Enough with your ramblings!' the man had said that day. 'How many bookings does she have? Clear them all. I'm having her all night long!' The pimp knew that no one would be able to refuse the charms of this young Peranakan woman, whose heritage was a mixture of Chinese and Sundanese. Especially since in Kramat Tunggak types like hers were hard to come by.

'We're closing soon. She's too tired. Anyway, she's a hot sell. You've gotta get in line until next week, buddy!'

'Get *your* arse in line! Here's your money, how much more do you need?'

'I don't want it, I'm not risking losing all my customers! You see this long list of bookings, all for her, until next week? Procedure is procedure, Mister!'

A loaded Colt 45 was cocked on the pimp's temple. 'I dare you to say procedure one more time,' the man barked.

The list fell from the pimp's hands.

That the man claimed to be the son of an army general was a well-known rumour among the pimps of Kramat Tunggak. That the rumour could be wrong is a possibility no pimp had ever tried looking into. In any case, the man had a gun with him now.

With the cold metal of the gun still on his forehead, the pimp shakily waved his hand towards the young woman watching them all the while from the corner of the room.

The new prima donna of Kramat Tunggak, wearing a thin see-through nightgown, didn't even bat an eyelid. Strangely, she was quite fascinated by this punter, apparently willing to kill for her.

So that was their first meeting.

Their encounter began with her mother's outstretched hand to the man, who immediately responded by pushing her to the wall and thrusting his hungry lips on hers, followed by endless kisses all over her body. With the shaken pimp still watching, she couldn't help letting a weak moan escape her lips while the man sucked on her ample breasts, and as she collapsed into his arms, he readily carried her to bed.

The lovemaking that night was the wildest, most intense, and most pleasurable she had ever experienced. 'Two hours non-stop, followed by another two hours,' her mother recalled softly. A first impression she had yet to find with any other man.

In one breath her mother summarised their entire relationship: dates upon dates under the moonlight in the car park of Senen Station, peck upon peck on her lips, silly jokes that never failed to make her laugh atop the pedicab they rode in, dinners at fancy restaurants, and lovemaking sessions that grew ever wilder with time.

Since she started going out with that man, she felt disgusted by other punters who took so long to finish, and would just lie there in satisfaction afterwards, taking forever to leave. She started to treat them coldly.

No longer did she massage her clients' dicks with oil to make them last longer. No longer did she go out with the other girls to shop for traditional aromatherapy concoctions to steam and tighten their pussies. She even refused the *Amor Rose* or *Shanghai Lotion* that was offered to her for free.

She never understood how the other girls, who also had boyfriends or kept a lover, could still serve their customers with the same lust and desire.

Her clients might be satisfied – climaxing so hard they projectile cummed all over the mattress – but she never felt as whole as she did with her man. While the client screamed in satisfaction, she would stare blankly at the bedroom ceiling, fantasising about her boyfriend's face.

Presents from him came flooding in, dozens and dozens of fake Wacoal panties and Triumph bras, Mirabella lipsticks, and see-through bed gowns, as well as hungry kisses every time he visited. All made her desperate to quit her job.

This time her daughter took a deep breath. 'Enough. Enough with the sex stories,' she pleaded. 'Focus on how bad he was to you. Don't dwell on the good parts.'

Her mother acceded, continuing to what happened two years later.

The pimp, who was famous for never losing a single game of chess, was sitting, frozen, in his house's waiting room. It had been almost four hours, and he was still being besieged by those damned pawns. Even after a pack of kretek cigarettes and three cups of black coffee, he was still unable to move.

'Check mate.'

That night, he lost. Reflexively the pimp banged on the table.

As part of their deal, the young bastard got to take home his most treasured diva. He had sixty girls, and was willing to lose any of them but her.

It was especially painful because the man who took her away was her good-for-nothing boyfriend, who did nothing but swindle people right and left, gamble every cent he had, and was often found passed out drunk on the streets after fucking random whores in Kramat Tunggak. He knew his favourite girl often used her tips to go on dates and sleep with the bastard. And now she was leaving with him.

'Fetch me some water. Water!' The bastard instructed. When the prettiest woman in his brothel went to obey him, he felt his blood boiling.

But at the time her mother felt ecstatic for being able to choose her own path, for once.

The two of them started to live together – beginning six years filled with endless wild desires that never stopped giving.

'So you chose the guy just because you had great fucking sessions?'

Her mother smiles bitterly. 'In the car park, at the cinema, in the Tirta Mas swimming pool, on the hospital stairs, at the TIM backstage, behind the mosque, in a church toilet…'

She closed her eyes and sighed, giving up. Her mother stopped listing all their hook-up spots. When she opened her eyes, while heaving a big sigh, she inquired, 'And, of course, both of you never expected me?'

Her mother took a breath.

She glared at the woman in disgust, faintly taking a step back, 'Did he want a kid? He wanted me?'

Her mother shook her head.

Thank goodness. She had never been wanted by the man who was never in her life.

Despite quitting her job, they had continued to rent a house in the Kramat Tunggak area. Her mother stopped selling her body and contributed to their household by doing people's laundry, while her lover gradually became more and more useless. When her mother began to want a child, the man paid no interest and started causing trouble on purpose. Once, he brought home a few women and forced them into an orgy. Another time he let her get groped by another man just so he could pay off a debt. Once, he came home drunk, banging on the door like a madman and vomited all over her the moment she opened the door.

With each of his intolerable words and acts, she wanted to leave even more, but time and time again she failed.

When she realised that she was pregnant, knowing that he'd force her into an abortion, her mother grew more desperate. She knew that the only way the baby she was carrying would be safe, and that she would be free, was if the man was dead or imprisoned.

Listening to her mother's story, she gulped down as much water as she could. 'So, because you sent him to jail, he now wants to seek us out and kill us? What did you do?'

All tragedies, in their own way, have a silver lining. One day he came home drunk with a friend, who went into her mother's bedroom and demanded her services. She refused, and he hit her. The stranger then forcefully pinned her down, while she struggled underneath his plump body. Her screams grew even louder when her lover came and pulled his friend off her — only to be dumbstruck by the sight of his friend covered in blood, a pair of scissors jabbed into his neck.

She was stunned into silence and gave her mother a searching look.

'You killed him?'

Her mother closed her eyes – the answer to her question.

They sat in silence. The leftover rice and lodeh soup sat sadly on their plates. Only the sound of the humming air conditioner and the ticking clock filled the room.

'And you laid the blame on him?'

This time, she was answered by a hug, her mother's arms desperately tightening up around her. She felt something wet on her shoulder.

Note

1. Lapo: a Batak-style restaurant.

Grown-Up Kids

Ziggy Zezsyazeoviennazabrizkie

Translated by Annie Tucker

Mrs M cooked lontong sayur for breakfast. Her husband came and sat down and said, 'Oh!' He rubbed his tummy, laughing. 'It's been a long time.'

Mrs M made Indomie fried noodles for Mr M's packed lunch, and prepared his adult nappy.

★

Early that same morning, Mrs O sat by the side of the road and flagged down the first chicken porridge cart she saw. She didn't answer the moustachioed peddler's questions, so he went ahead and put all the porridge, chicken pieces, fried soya beans, chopped spring onions and crispy fried shallots in one plastic bag, the yellow chicken broth in another plastic bag, the fried crackers in another plastic bag, then put all those plastic bags inside another plastic bag, and gave it to Mrs O. Her hand trembled as she paid. It was cheap. The thought of it made Mrs O feel nauseous.

Mrs N found Mrs O half an hour later still standing in the same place with the porridge uneaten. From the front door, Mrs N whispered loudly for Mrs O to come in. When Mrs O got to the door, Mrs N said that she wasn't going to eat that. Just because today was the last day, it didn't mean she had to act crazy.

'Yeah,' said Mrs O, 'but if not now, when?'

★

On the morning of the second Tuesday in November, a 40-passenger bus was idling in the street of their housing complex, ready to take 37 senior citizens to the amusement park on the outskirts of the city. As he was escorting his wife to the bus, Mr M shuddered. Mrs M assumed the lontong sayur and vegetables from earlier that morning were starting to irritate her husband's bowels, so held back a moment to distance herself from a rumbling fart, but then remembered their plans for the day. 'Do you have everything you need?' the couple asked each other, and then exchanged nods that only they could fully understand. Mr M let Mrs M pull away from him, then sat down at the edge of the garden and ordered an Uber. He watched pensively as his wife was swallowed up by the bus.

Mr and Mrs M had met in the street as two college students running from a tear gas attack. Mrs M grabbed his hand and dragged him through the crowd towards clear air. The next day they'd met again, and Mr M had given her a bottle of water and some Sari Roti buns. In her backpack, Mrs M had been carrying three packages of buns – chocolate, chocolate-cheese, and chocolate-srikaya – but she didn't tell him. When Mr M then went missing for two days, Mrs M had searched the internet and figured out his full name and identity. She'd visited Mr M in the hospital. After the demonstrations came to an end, Mr M invited Mrs M to the National Library for a Sari Roti picnic. They then gathered material for their final research projects, Mrs M from the multimedia floor, Mr M from the archives. Mr M got a job at the library after graduation, while Mrs M worked as an expert mechanic in factories and service centres, before landing her dream job at the amusement park. When she was promoted to Dufan's[1] head mechanic, Mrs M invited Mr M to ride the roller coasters in the middle of the night and they got engaged on Halilintar's peak.

As the bus was driving away, Mrs M noticed a black car rolling into their housing complex. Maybe it was the car that would pick up her husband, she thought. Mr M was also a member of the senior citizen association, but Mrs M had suggested that they do it separately. She didn't want to see her husband like that, and she didn't want him to see her like that either. When Mr M had first agreed, she had wept. 'Mr M's not coming?' people asked. 'He has some work to do,' said Mrs M. Nobody asked again because they knew how important getting any kind of work was for old folks like them.

There were lots of seniors in this complex. Almost all the houses were owned by old folks who had bought before the price of land skyrocketed, with only a few being rented out. This small portion was occupied by busy young people, who moved in and then moved on just as quickly, and didn't have the time to stop and chat. So, the only ones who knew each other were the elderly who tried to stave off their loneliness and senility with morning strolls, hoping to run into an acquaintance or two. One December, ten years ago, Mr R had suggested they form a senior citizen association. Mrs P ridiculed him the whole afternoon.

Today was their day for going out and about; they had a set schedule for this twice a year so that they all didn't die of boredom. And it just so happened, a few months ago, Mr T's grandson had told him that after today, Istana Boneka would be closed for good. Not everyone immediately agreed to go there – the park had been open since their parents' time, and no one cared about its outdated mechanical figures. But then they all thought it over: a lot was always happening there, whether it was happening to them or not – West Javanese college students, new to the city, who spent weekends riding Tornado and Kora-Kora, shouting the expletives really meant for their professors; little kids who had yet to experience anything more interesting; city dwellers bored with the shopping mall; parents who were out of ideas; bickering teenage couples with snickering boys who called their girlfriends scaredy-cats, and the girlfriends who retorted that the rides were supposed to be scary and it was perfectly normal to scream and anyone who didn't should probably go see a doctor.

So, in the end, they agreed to give Istana Boneka a final salute.

Inside the bus, Mrs N trembled in her seat. Being out and about made her nervous, especially when sitting atop a set of spinning wheels. She had been like this ever since she was young. Mrs N came from a village whose total population wasn't even as large as the number of passengers in one of the KRL train cars she used to ride on her commute. As a young woman, she had been besieged by crowds and she had endured it all – the dizziness, the smell, the wandering hands – for money. In the middle of a city that was bustling even though it had been abandoned, Mrs N – even now that she was all grown-up – was still terrified. Because of all that, Mrs P's idea sounded excellent to Mrs N. She could finally find the peace she yearned for. No one should have to live like that, especially not someone as old as she was. If only she didn't have to go out to do it… if only… But she couldn't do it alone inside her house. If Mrs P was there, maybe she could strengthen her resolve – or at least mock her until she couldn't take it anymore. Mrs P was an expert at that.

What's more, because of her anxiety, Mrs N had never made it to the amusement park before. Much like other people who moved to the city from elsewhere, visiting it was a dream of hers. But whenever her friends from the village came to visit and invited her to go, she always said no, she couldn't make it, she had no time, she was busy, she was sick. Now was the time. The time had come. It was now or never. It had been too long.

Behind Mrs N was Mrs O. She was clutching her lunch box tightly. She had prepared its contents herself; clean food, nutritious. It was true what Mrs N had said; just because today was the last day didn't mean she had to act stupid. She wanted to scold Mrs M for preparing an instant noodle lunch for her husband's last meal, but she realised there was no longer any use in harping on about other people's diet.

In her youth, Mrs O's friends had had enough money to adopt a certain lifestyle: one with raw honey, quinoa salad and hydroponic vegetables, kombucha with chia seeds, mixed dried fruit and granola scooped into fashionable paper bags… All the more expensive because they were 'healthier'. Mrs O had a weak heart and lots of money, so she followed the trend. To this day, the only thing she spread on her bread was *'homemade almond butter'*. Mrs O no longer ate gado-gado from roadside stalls, but *'all-organic vegan poke bowls with brown rice, konjac jelly and seaweed with Himalayan salt'*. There was no more squeezed juice from street vendors, just *'cold-pressed juice, no added sugar'*.

Unfortunately, the weakness of Mrs O's heart was no joke. After a while, the 'healthy' labels began to haunt her more with every passing day. There was smoke on the street corner – she would die of air pollution. There was dust on her plate – she would be devoured by bacteria. Somebody sneezed – she would be killed by a foreign virus. Like a well-worn pair of shoes, her anxiety walked with her wherever she went. Before she was even thirty years old, she had heart disease and high blood pressure. 'Because my life isn't healthy enough,' she said on the way home from yoga class. It was exhausting to live engulfed by fear.

'Hey,' Mrs P poked Mrs O's arm twice, her face insolent. 'When was your *first time?*'

Mrs O tried not to wince, but it was hard. Mrs P – like many kids who grew up with western films and internet culture – was accustomed to using English. Mrs O had been like that too, but now she was fully grown. She didn't want to bring it up, but she also really wanted Mrs P to stop.

Yes, she thought, and soon enough she will stop.

'Six, or seven,' she replied. Mrs O had been born outside the city, but her father often went to Jakarta for work. Once she was big enough, she flew in her first aeroplane on her first vacation, and the amusement park had been the destination. Istana Boneka was the attraction she most wanted to visit, but the queue to get in was very long. Her mother said, wait until the afternoon, then kept repeating that while dragging her from one ride to another. But afternoon came and went, and the queue was still quite long and until this very day, Mrs O hadn't yet set foot inside Istana Boneka. As they approached the ride she thought this over and realised that she never would.

In an effort to make some small talk, Mrs O asked Mrs P when she'd first visited the amusement park. Mrs P waved her hand dismissively. 'Probably *around the same time.* I've forgotten.' Mrs O winced again. She had abandoned the code-switching culture some time in her forties. That was for kids, she thought, with the arrogance of a 'cultured' and 'mature' adult. Mrs P had no class.

But Mrs P always did have wild, interesting ideas. And this time, even she – Mrs O – had finally been sucked in. At first, Mrs O and Mrs N were both hesitant. But Mrs M agreed so quickly that they became intrigued, despite the fact that they knew the idea came from money trouble, which was not a problem for Mrs O, who had a significant inheritance, or Mrs N, who was rich off her pension.

Once the capital had been relocated and all the government offices moved, Jakarta was left with only historic buildings. In the hands of capitalists, those remnants had all been dressed up and the abandoned city quickly became a tourist magnet. Prices skyrocketed in the most-visited districts, but wages stayed practically the same. The young fought desperately to hold on. Old folks fell back on whatever savings they had left, and for those who didn't have a stable income, it became a struggle to survive.

Take Mr and Mrs M, for example – the older they got, the more destitute they became. They had long thought to move to another, friendlier city, open a small fish farm or something like that, but they could only save little bits here and there from the odd jobs they could find. It seemed that they would sooner die than be able to save up enough to move.

Mrs P couldn't figure out why no one wanted to buy Mr and Mrs M's house and was shocked to hear the explanation. 'But don't a lot of young people live in our complex? Meaning they can afford to buy our houses, right?'

'They're renting,' said Mrs O, who was herself surprised that Mrs P was surprised. In any case, the couple had long lived by credit culture – buy now, pay later – Mrs P must know about these things? 'These days, renting a big house for fifty years is cheaper than buying one small house. And that's before annual property taxes.'

This had been a blow to Mrs P who had only recently realised that she could no longer order in takeaway every day. She was so shaken that soon she fell ill. Her three friends said she wasn't *that* sick, but Mrs P was sure she was on death's door. Yet here she was, still alive, with all her savings spent on hospital bills.

Perhaps too late in the day, she began to regret her choice

of letting her husband move to the new capital by himself. At that time, stubbornly, Mrs P had chosen to stay in the luxurious house they had built when they were young. Her husband took the kids. Well, it was up to him. She was too fond of the carpet and the wallpaper and the heavy curtains. Her three children wanted nothing more to do with her. It was up to them; she preferred the back terrace where she and her lawyer cronies would smoke while working on cases. She never met her grandchildren. It was too bad, but it was up to them. People were free to choose, and, either way, her crystal chandelier couldn't leave the house.

When her money ran out, Mrs P started to panic because she had always thought that if it came to that, she would just be forced to sell her beloved home and go live in a house that was… ordinary. But if that didn't take care of her money worries… And if there wasn't even anyone who could afford to buy a mouldy old house like the one the M couple had… Now there was nothing she could do. She had stopped practising law a long time ago. Her old colleagues had either died or moved to the new capital, for their work or partners or kids. Mrs P had nothing left. Could it be that she might die, poor and sick, like a village beggar?

The afternoon Mrs P suggested a group suicide on their November outing, she entertained herself with the fantasy that people would come to see where the mastermind behind the crazy Dufan plot lived. Then, struck by the beauty of their home, one of these might even go so far as to seek out the family to put an offer in on the house. But then they'd discover that her husband had already died, the first child had rejected their inheritance, and it'd been over a year since her second child renounced her citizenship to live abroad with her husband, and therefore the land was now owned by the government. Ah, yes. Death would be her final, most entertaining lark.

★

'Hurry up, *bitch.*' Mrs P jabbed Mrs N's back with her finger. So impolite. Mrs O shook her head but didn't say anything, keeping her focus on tending to Mrs N who was having trouble breathing. Mrs M announced to the group that they would soon disembark and enter the park. The members of the group who had wanted to stretch their legs, hastily responded. Led by Mr T, they tottered towards the queue for Dufan. The final performance would be later in the afternoon, but the park was already starting to get crowded. From a distance, Mrs O thought that if she hadn't had a plan like this, she wouldn't be able to get in, with the queue as long as it was.

Mrs M received a text and when she opened it she found a message from her husband: he had arrived at the National Library. Mrs M didn't like the place; it was too big and too quiet. But Mr M relished its stillness, and as part of his poetic departure, he insisted he wanted to return to the location of their first date. Mrs M had blushed and blown her nose when she heard his plan.

Mr M was on the fifteenth floor now, the reference collection. Two security guards were pretending not to see him. He was waiting for lunchtime when the guards would go. There was no one else on that floor. Mr M had already eaten the fried noodles, which had congealed and gone cold, just like he used to eat when he was in school. After he prayed on the sixth floor, he sent a laughing emoji and a slightly bitter message regarding his last rites. At the amusement park, Mrs M clutched her phone as if it were her husband's hand.

Ten minutes later, they got off the bus. Mrs P lined them up in front of the gate to Hysteria. The four of them stood hunched in a sea of young kids. Mrs N was clinging on to Mrs O, Mrs M was clinging on to the memory of her husband, Mrs O was clutching her chest, her heart racing. They were all so anxious, on the verge of collapse.

But not Mrs P. Mrs P was humming, smiling to herself, thinking about the past and the non-existent future. The last time she had come here, dozens of years ago, she had been with her ex-husband and her ex-children. Some of the rides hadn't even been built yet. She liked Hysteria. She had forbidden her children to ride with her – she would go by herself, and her husband would mind the children down below – but they insisted. Her second child vomited halfway through. Those waiting in line were showered with barf, and those on the ride were smacked with chunks of sick while hurtling through the air. Mrs P had never laughed harder. When she was crafting her final prank, she knew the hilarious 'Vomit Comet' had to be the place.

They were stopped by an attendant who asked, 'Are you sure?' Mrs M snorted in amusement. She had certainly thought it over hard enough. Mrs P quickly pointed out that the rules of the ride only said 'minimum height 120cm'; there was no upper age limit. The man looked worried but, unable to muster a counterargument, he stepped aside and opened the gate. Mrs P grinned and yanked Mrs N through as fast as she could before the attendant could notice the panicked look on her face.

'Mrs P!' called Mrs O, who was already shaking. They had taken their seats and were waiting for the other riders to get strapped in. 'What if you fail?' She looked at Mrs P, who glared back. 'You're not as sick as all that.'

'I will not fail,' Mrs P spluttered. Her eyes bulged wider. 'I *am* that sick. I had to stay in the hospital, don't you know! I spent all my money on treatment! *Why don't you shut up, just because you're also sick doesn't mean you're a doctor!*'

Mrs O did not reply. The queue gate was closed; the last riders were already seated and the ride was about to start.

Mrs M looked at the safety harness, which had not changed at all over the years. She knew it very well. She smiled and stroked the nuts and bolts with a familiarity that made her quietly weep. From her skirt pocket, she took out a screwdriver. Mrs N peeked over from the seat beside her but was too terrified to speak – oh there were so many people around. Next to her, Mrs O was weak, pale, still, and silent. On the end, Mrs P stamped her feet and fidgeted like an excited little kid.

The attendant gave the signal indicating the ride was about to begin. Mrs M closed her eyes, drew a breath. Mrs N squeezed her harness so tightly her fingernails turned white. Mrs O blinked. Mrs P began to sing *'I am a rock I am an i-i-i-i-island'*. Mr M, on the fifteenth floor of the National Library, opened a large window in the archives and looked down, remembering the street he had trodden with his friends in his youth, the spot where they had blocked traffic, angry about proposed laws, about people, about human rights violations, about sausages (and whether there was pork in them) – the spot where he had first met his wife wearing a red jacket and carrying a knapsack that, he knew, held three packages of buns. He had taken that road to his first job. His wife had often picked him up on that street to drive him home. Mr M closed his eyes, drew a breath.

The ride began its ascent. Mrs M let out a shrill laugh. Then the oversized toy shot towards the sky at a speed of 100 km/hour. In the first second, Mrs M's behind was lifted from her seat and went flying, like eggs and flour being tossed at a birthday party. In the second second, still laughing, she let go of her screwdriver, dropped her cell phone. At the National Library, Mr M jumped. In the third second, the ride began to descend too. Mrs O made no sound.

Mrs N screamed. Her screams were never-ending, louder than any sound that had ever been; as if the park visitors and employees had all crammed into her mouth and then screamed out their prayers through a loudspeaker, like the adzan who gave everyone a headache, but no one could complain about for fear of going to jail – ah, yes, when she was young, Mrs N had signed a petition about this case; what had ever happened with that? In that same third second, Mrs N couldn't think. The old woman beside her – red cardigan, light brown skirt, grey hair – suddenly disappeared like skewers of satay when the day's fasting ended. And below – below – there were more people than before. Mrs N was going to die. Die on the ride or die because there were just so many people, she didn't know which, but she had the feeling she was going to die. Yes Lord, she was going to die… She had in fact come here to die, hadn't she?

Then, something happened to Mrs N. Something in her brain was awakened by the scream, and seemed to join in as her body, too, accelerated – Mrs N felt like a leopard! Strong as a bull! So fired up! So hot! – and then suddenly stopped.

Just like that. Mrs N had screamed herself to death.

The ride reached its full height again on the sixth second. Mrs P looked over to her left. Two had died in their seats, one had died – somewhere, but with her skull crushed and her body strewn about in pieces, that foolish Mrs M. Down below, the attendants turned pale and blamed each other. Who had forgotten to fasten the old lady's safety harness? Why hadn't someone pushed the emergency button? How fast could the ride be stopped? *We're all screwed*. Mrs P looked straight ahead and smiled wide. She was the last. Her turn was next. The ride's camera took a picture of her smiling. She looked quite beautiful next to the corpses of her two friends. *Let's die.*

The ride slowed down, then stopped. People ripped off their seatbelts and still screaming – in fact, screaming louder – went running in different directions, checking to see who was dead and who was vomiting on Hysteria. In the end, as befitting its name, the ride had made dozens of people scream and cry. A group of tourists whispered that the old woman who had been flung from the ride landed next to a little kid who was tasting rujak cireng for the first time at the Dermaga Marina. Hearing that, more people spewed their guts.

Mrs P slumped forward out of her seat and staggered toward the exit. She was still alive. Her entire body shook with rage and resentment. She had been the one to think all this up, being of above average intelligence, but she was the one who had failed to die. Damn it!

Her photo was available for purchase at the counter. Mrs N's hands were folded in her lap with her head bowed, oh so sweet even in death. Mrs O looked like an ugly squashed grasshopper, her eyes crossed and her mouth agape. Mrs M – Mrs P laughed – wasn't there. She purchased the photo, then left.

She bought some water and sat under a garden umbrella. Her hands were still trembling. She looked at Hysteria – all operations had been halted, and people were starting to swarm the area. What should she do? She couldn't go home; she had no money to pay this month's electricity bill. Or maybe she might, if she didn't buy her favourite shrimp pasta and creamy bisque… But she had just been saved from death; shouldn't she celebrate?

Now *that* was a ride that didn't require a minimal height, she thought, glaring at the spinning cups – what was that ride called, Teapots? *They're cups, dummy, not pots.* Ah, a cheap bottle of iced tea would be refreshing about now – a shame that more expensive tea was only sold by snobs these days. Yes, *that* was a ride that was safe for the elderly, that and stupid Dufan. But had they ever even considered that some ornery old folks with advanced heart disease might try their luck on one of the more adrenaline-spiking rides? No! Grown-ups and tall people could think more clearly, maybe that's what they were thinking. Short ones are closer to the fumes of stinky feet.

Yes, but they were so wrong, these stupid capitalists. They were so eager to let as many people as possible on their washed-up ride, they forgot they were supposed to protect their visitors. That was unforgivable. She had lost her three best friends today, and all because an amusement park didn't have clear rules or adequate protection for people who were sick or elderly, who might be getting senile.

Well, it's still a bit disorganised, thought Mrs P. But she could refine her argument later, when she sued for pain and suffering.

Notes

1. Dufan (also known as Dunia Fantasi): an amusement park located in North Jakarta on the sea front. It is part of Taman Impian Jaya Ancol (Ancol Dreamland), a resort that includes an international championship golf course, hotels and other recreational facilities.

Haji Syiah

Ben Sohib

Translated by Paul Agusta

THE KAMPONG OF MELAYU Pulo is definitely not the only kampong in Jakarta where you will find both clerics and drunks, but it is entirely possible that it's the only place that you can find two drunken young men and a cleric in the same gazebo during a prayer group. Even though you can't really call it a prayer group. Despite the cleric slipping in parables and bits of sermon, the prayer group is more of a relaxed place to talk about random things, a place where thoughts are traded, and jokes are shared late into the night. But for the purpose of this tale we are telling, we will still refer to it as a prayer group.

Whoever decides to stroll through our kampong on any sunny afternoon will immediately notice that this area is indeed the residence of many clerics. From their very first step, any visitor will see a cleric sitting on his porch. On their second step, they will find a cleric standing by the side of the street adjusting his sarong, and another cleric removing his white hat to scratch his head. If the visitor is lucky, on their fourth and fifth step, they might catch one of these clerics pinching the leg of the lady selling gado-gado.

Come sundown, the clerics will be seen walking – individually or in groups – towards the Assalam Musala to perform the Maghrib prayer together. After prayers, they will return to their homes. One of them is known by the name Haji Syiah. After dinner and the Isya prayer, the clerics will yawn several times before finally falling asleep and starting to snore, still wrapped in their sarongs; except for Haji Syiah.

Haji Syiah will be seen sitting on his porch, welcoming the participants of his prayer group, which includes Faruk and Ketel, a pair of friends that almost always arrive in various states of inebriation. Haji Syiah never picks favourites among his guests; the sober and the intoxicated are treated equally. The same coffee is poured out to all, the same cassava chips and peanuts shared round, and the same clove cigarettes offered. Thus, the prayer group always manages to have an atmosphere of warmth.

The news of Faruk and Ketel joining the prayer group at Haji Syiah's house spread to all denizens of the kampong, including Haji Jamil, a most respected cleric. Without wasting any time, a mere day after hearing the news, Haji Jamil felt the need to reprimand Haji Syiah. Directly after the Maghrib prayer at the Musala Assalam, in front of the entire congregation, Haji Jamil spoke.

'It's not proper, Haji, allowing drunkards to gather at your house like that.'

'I am not in the business of gathering drunkards, but I will never refuse guests who come to my house. I will even welcome drunks. Their drinking is their business to take up with Allah, as long as they don't bother the neighbours. If they're rowdy drunks, whether they drink on my porch or they drink on any street corner of the kampong, I will kick their asses!' replied Haji Syiah with his small childlike fist punching the air, failing to intimidate anyone.

Haji Saku could not contain his laughter, even with his hand firmly cupping his mouth. The same goes for Haji Sahrudin, Haji Rozak, and several other clerics. Haji Munip had the worst fate, before his hands could even attempt to stifle his laughter, it escaped in a loud uncontrollable guffaw. Who could not laugh at the thought of Haji Syiah, this frail and tiny cleric, attempting to beat up a couple of drunken young men?

Well-known is the tale of Haji Syiah being so small and light that he was once knocked on to his behind by the gust of a motorcycle whizzing by. He was standing by the side of the road when a rowdy teenager drove by so fast that the wind from the bike caused Haji Syiah's lithe form to spin a full 180 degrees and fall into a sitting position on the ground. Haji Syiah sprang up, waving his fists in the air and yelling, 'You're lucky you didn't hit me! If you had, I'd tear you to pieces!'

Tear the young driver into pieces? Even a slight gust of wind knocked him on his ass, what would happen if he got hit... was the thought that crossed the mind of the Neighbourhood Association Leader who witnessed the incident. This drove the Leader to order the construction of a speed bump made of sand and cement on the street so similar incidents wouldn't occur. This was the myth behind the existence of the speed bump right in front of Haji Syiah's home. No one really knows who started this legend. Of course, no one actually believes that it ever happened, no matter how thin and small Haji Syiah may be. What is certain is that the story has caused much laughter throughout the kampong.

So it comes as no surprise that Haji Sakur, Haji Sahrudin, Haji Rozak, and Haji Munip (he was the loudest) failed to contain their composure when Haji Syiah started waving his tiny fists in the air in a threatening manner. The thought of him falling on his rear end immediately came to mind.

Throughout the year that Haji Syiah had welcomed Faruk and Ketel into his home, not a single kampong had seen their faith diminish. Life went on the way it always did, no better, no worse. In other words, except for Haji Jamil, no one felt that what Haji Syiah did was inappropriate. In fact, it made them happy because ever since Faruk and Ketel joined Haji Syiah's prayer group, they no longer got drunk and caused trouble in the kampong.

Before, amongst the numerous drunks in the kampong, Faruk and Ketel were known to be the rowdiest. They had a reputation for never stopping until they fell unconscious. Every night they would buy cheap moonshine in Pisangan Lama, near Jatinegara Station. Word has it that, between the two of them, they could polish off 10 litres every night. On the first litre of alcohol, they would still speak using 'ane' and 'ente'[1] like any proper Arab-Indonesian. On the second litre, they would start speaking in polite Indonesian, complete with 'saya' and 'anda'.[2] On the third litre, they would heavily argue with each other in English, even though only the Devil and themselves knew exactly what they were talking about. From the fourth litre onward, they would start running around the kampong, screaming at the top of their lungs.

It was during one of these bouts of late-night shenanigans when Haji Syiah, sitting comfortably on his porch, suddenly leapt up and approached them. He rolled his sarong high; his unbuttoned shirt showed his protruding ribs under wrinkled skin. He didn't even put on his white cleric's cap, which caused his nearly bald head to glisten in the moonlight.

'If the two of you make one more sound, I'll slit your throats!' bellowed Haji Syiah.

Haji Syiah posed for an attack, both his knees slightly bent, his right palm cupped facing up, his left hand behind his head as if he were propping it up. No one really knew if Haji Syiah was an expert in martial arts, but legend had it, he had mastered the magical 'Mystic Sword' move that could knock an opponent down from far away. Although this legend had been long believed by the kampong people, no one really

76

knew who started it. But of course, this piece of lore had been partially discredited by the widespread anecdote about Haji Syiah falling on his rear end from a speeding motorcycle whizzing past him.

Even with all things considered, seeing Haji Syiah ready to pounce, coupled with the threat to cut their throat, Faruk and Ketel rose to their feet. Whether it was due to alcohol or studying under the wrong master, their stances appeared more than slightly off: legs spread too far apart, and arms too far forward.

Their fighting stances may have been laughable, but the moment was still quite tense. Aren't drunken folks known to do unpredictable things? Definitely! Faruk started to feel behind his belt for something. A knife, maybe? Meanwhile, his best friend Ketel remained in his ridiculous fighting stance, struggling to keep his balance. Haji Syiah grew more vigilant.

Unwilling to risk defeat, Haji Syiah began to bust out the 'Mystic Sword', his lips spitting out prayers. It is believed that once the prayers had been read three times, a single breath was enough to make your opponents collapse and fall to their knees. Without wasting another moment, Haji Syiah took a deep breath and blew hard at the faces of the two thugs. It was at that moment that Haji Syiah's false teeth went flying out of his mouth. The teeth flew through the air and fell by his opponents' feet. Silence fell suddenly, as if the night itself held its breath.

Faruk and Ketel looked at each other. Suddenly, the two drunkards exploded into laughter, doing everything in their power not to roll on the ground in hysterics. They laughed so hard; their stomachs hurt. Faruk and Ketel kept laughing, louder and louder, their bellies stiffening. Finally, they fell on their knees in front of Haji Syiah.

Faruk and Ketel kissed Haji Syiah's hand. They tried so hard to apologise, but with every word they said, the next word would be drowned by laughter, tears falling down their faces. Fortunately, once Haji Syiah stroked their foreheads, the laughter of the two drunkards subsided, saving them from life-threatening stomach cramps.

Since that incident, Faruk and Ketel repented. Never again did they cause trouble in the kampong, although they continued to consume about ten litres of moonshine a night. The pair of them even became the most loyal members of Haji Syiah's prayer group. One could say that they even became Haji Syiah's favourites, if there were such a thing.

The troublemaking twosome of Faruk and Ketel no longer causing disturbances in the kampong and becoming Haji Syiah's favourites were clear, solid facts. But whether or not the details of the tale of the drunkards − especially the part about the ridiculous fighting stance and false teeth flying through the air − were entirely true was open to question, due to the fact that the story came from the mouth of Ucup Bodong, the snack vendor who claimed to see the incident as he was closing up shop. He allegedly witnessed the entire scene from behind his stall. Faruk and Ketel themselves would always keep schtum every time they were asked. Meanwhile, no one had the heart to ask Haji Syiah directly for clarification.

Haji Syiah is in his sixties. His real name is Rohili. They call him Haji Syiah not because he follows the Syiah[3] teachings. The way he practices his faith is no different than the rest of the kampong. It is possible that the name came about because of the large poster of Ayatollah Khomeini on his living room wall, next to a photo of Habib Ali Kwitang.[4] Once, twenty years ago, after Haji Syiah came home from his Haj pilgrimage, Haji Jamil paid a visit to his home. It was in that moment Haji Jamil advised him to take down the poster of the Ayatollah.

'Why did you put up that poster?' Haji Jamil said, pointing at the image of the Ayatollah. 'He is a Shiite, he is not like us.'

'It doesn't matter if he's different. I just like looking at his face,' answered Haji Syiah calmly.

So, it is quite possible that the nickname originated from the mouth of Haji Jamil. Either way, it spread throughout the kampong, from the mouth of a resident to the ears of another resident. Although no one would dare to call him Haji Syiah to his face, the cleric is very aware that is what people call him. And he does not mind it.

Haji Syiah lived with Nyak Mun, his wife. Together, they have spent more than forty years patiently sailing through life's lonely ocean. In the first five to ten years of their marriage, they – especially Haji Syiah – still hoped for the presence of a child (he wanted a son) that would brighten up their home. But, as the years passed, they slowly buried that dream, deeper and deeper. It is unclear on exactly which year of their marriage this happened, but they finally accepted their fate as a childless couple.

'God didn't give us one,' was always how Haji Syiah answered every time someone asked how many kids he had. Haji Syiah had fully accepted his fate, but deep down in his heart of hearts, his desire for fatherhood was never fully quelled. This desire would appear in the form of his interest in helping young people. In the middle of his prayer group, he was known to occasionally say, 'If God had given me a child, he'd be your age by now.'

It was as if Haji Syiah saw echoes of the son of his dreams in the young men in his prayer group, even the drunken ones. It is actually towards the drunken ones that he felt the most affection. He looked at Faruk and Ketel the way a father would look at his sons. As gently as he could, he pulled the two young men from the grip of the cheap alcohol that he felt could harm their health as well as their futures.

'If you want to drink, drink in moderation. If you drink too much, where is the fun? Anyway, how long do you want to do this for? God loses nothing by the two of you getting drunk every day, you're the ones that stand to lose everything, your bodies will be ruined, your minds destroyed. You must think about your futures,' advised Haji Syiah one day.

In the months that followed, Faruk and Ketel continued to come to Haji Syiah's inebriated. But it's true what people say about enlightenment from God coming quickly and from unexpected directions. Who could have guessed that Faruk and Ketel would change into different people so quickly? Only seven months after they said goodbye to Haji Syiah to go work at an internet café owned by Ustad[5] Jaiz in Pandeglang, Faruk and Ketel reappeared at the kampong looking completely different. They wore long-sleeved dress shirts, dress pants hanging just above the ankle, and had black marks on their forehead, a sign of frequent prayer. Their moustaches were completely shaved, while their beards were grown out.

According to talk amongst the people of the kampong, while in Pandeglang, they diligently joined the prayer meetings at Ustad Jaiz's religious school, not far from the internet café they worked at. Ustad Jaiz, who was a distant cousin of Faruk, built the school, as well as several businesses like the internet café and a rice supply store in Pandeglang about a year before, after he finished his Sharia studies in Mecca. It had also been said that in a few days, Faruk and Ketel were to return to Pandeglang to join an intensive six-month course at Ustad Faiz's school before departing for Mecca. It was in that holy city – using the scholarship they got from the good relationship Ustad Jaiz had with a religious institution in Saudi Arabia – that they were to deepen their knowledge of Islam.

Of course, this news brought so much joy to Haji Syiah. He wanted so badly to meet up with Faruk and Ketel. A week had passed since their return from Pandeglang, but the two of them still hadn't gone to visit Haji Syiah at his home. Haji Syiah ended up meeting Faruk and Ketel one afternoon, exactly ten days after their arrival. By accident, Haji Syiah crossed their path in front of Yong Put's store. He did not recognise them at first. Only after their eyes met for two or three seconds did Haji Syiah joyfully yell out 'Faruk! Ketel!'

The owners of the names would not respond. They turned their heads and continued on their way after one of them, Faruk, spat on the ground. This shocked Haji Syiah into silence, stopping him in his tracks, staring at their backs as they faded out of view. A thousand questions circled in his mind, he could not understand what was going on.

The thousand questions continued to plague his thoughts, as he sat on his porch. Why did Faruk and Ketel do that to him? Could it have been because they felt they had been reborn as holy, and therefore felt shame for their less-than-holy past? Or was there another reason? Haji Syiah could not find the answer.

Suddenly, Haji Syiah felt very tired. He leaned his head against the wall and closed his eyes. When he opened his eyes a few minutes later, Haji Syiah faintly saw what may have been Faruk and Ketel opening his front gate and drunkenly walking across the yard. Haji Syiah rubbed his eyes. The wind blew awfully hard that night, causing a branch to break off from the starfruit tree that grew in the yard.

Notes

1. Ane is 'Me/I' and Ente is 'You' in Arab-Indonesian dialect, originating from the Arabic 'Ana' (I/Me) and 'Anta/Antum' (You).

2. 'Saya' is 'I/Me' and 'Anda' is 'You' in formal Indonesian language.

3. Syiah or Shia Islam is one of the two main branches or teachings of Islam. It holds that the Prophet Muhammad designated Ali Ibn Abi Thalib as his successor. In Indonesia, the Shia Muslim are an often oppressed minority, because it is considered a sacrilegious deviation of the majority Sunni Muslim teachings.

4. Habib Ali bin Abdurrahman al-Habshi (1870–1968) or most known as Habib Ali Kwitang was one of the leading and groundbreaking Muslim clerics in Jakarta (then Batavia) Indonesia.

5. Another word for Cleric or religious teacher.

The Sun Sets in the North

Cyntha Hariadi

Translated by Eliza Vitri Handayani

THE FIRST TIME TATA saw her, Ace was kissing a boy in an empty classroom. Tata was stunned. Her legs stiffened as if she were the one caught in the act. Ace broke off the kiss, grabbed her bag, and left the classroom. Tata wondered if Ace had heard her heart clanging as loudly as the school bell behind her. She was certain Ace would yell at her. But, without even a single glance, Ace walked calmly out the school gate and into the car waiting for her.

Another voice stole Tata's attention, 'Why are you still here? Isn't your driver waiting for you?'

It was Ronny, the boy Ace had been kissing. Tata knew his name because their science teacher always thanked him for donating an unlimited supply of batteries from his family's company to the school laboratory. Tata left Ronny without a reply.

On the bus ride home, Tata replayed the incident in her head. *The nerve of that girl! What if a teacher saw her? Isn't kissing after school hours forbidden? Has that girl no shame?*

Tata had felt ashamed when she saw it, but now she just felt stupid for being so impressed by Ace's audacity – that was something she didn't have. Even after two years of knowing Ace, Tata still admired her. Not only had Ace had many boyfriends over the years, but she was also top of her class – like Tata was top of hers – and was always kind to everyone.

A week after Tata had seen her kissing Ronny, Ace finally spoke to her. Tata was walking to the bus stop after school and a car slowed down beside her. Ace's face appeared behind the lowered window.

'Hi, it's Renata, right? I'm Grace, but I go by Ace. Where you headed?'

Tata said she was going home. Ace immediately opened the car door and pulled her in. The din of the street vanished as soon as the door was closed, as if Tata had entered another world. Ace's friendly disposition quelled the awkwardness Tata was feeling from being in a quiet car with soft seats. Tata caught the driver's probing glance in the rearview mirror, he was wearing a stiff well-ironed safari suit. Tata was worried she might smell bad, but Ace didn't seem to notice.

'You saw me kissing a boy at school, but didn't gossip about me. You must be a nice person, Renata.'

'Just call me Tata,' she said.

They began talking about teachers, music, films, magazines, and the boys at school. The journey from school in Tanjung Duren to Tata's house in Mangga Besar only took half an hour, but by the end of it, both girls felt they had known each other for years.

Tata thought Ace would feel uncomfortable at her house, considering it was on a narrow street flanked by small houses all squashed together – but Ace seemed very relaxed talking to her parents and neighbours. Ace's driver would park by the side of a bigger road around the corner and wait for her.

Even though Ace's house in Pantai Mutiara was the same distance from school as Tata's, she always preferred to hang out or do homework at Tata's rather than hers. Tata was happy to have Ace over, although she was also curious about Ace's house. According to her father, Ace's family lived in one of the most exclusive housing complexes in Jakarta. The homeowners there not only had rights to the land, but also the sea. The sun set in the north there, her father would say – the rich made it that way so they could watch the sunset with the sea as the perfect backdrop.

Tata pictured Ace's room with a window facing the sea, which let Ace's imagination fly free, never crashing into the high walls of the Mangga Besar buildings. The sun never touched Tata's room, except just before nightfall, leaving giant shadows as a reminder for her to turn on the lights.

Tata's parents owned a small convenience store next to their house. Ace enjoyed helping Tata serve the customers. 'I remember when I was a kid, I used to love playing with my toy cash register, counting all my pretend money, but this time it's real, Ta, it's way more exciting!'

Ace often bought one or two items, from crackers and soaps to badminton rackets and bathroom scales – she said she needed them, but Tata doubted that. She took a handful of Ace's favourite milk candy, with a drawing of a rabbit on its wrapper, from the jar and gave it to her for free.

Ace also liked to play with the little chicks in Tata's backyard. As a side business, Tata's mother sold raw or cooked chicken with rujak sauce or turmeric seasoning. Ace often ordered from her as well. She said her family really liked the chicken. Tata doubted that as well, but felt no need to question it further – the most important thing was that her mother's cooking was selling well. Tata's parents agreed that Ace was a good friend.

The moment that really brought them together was when they lay side by side in Tata's bed, talking about Ace's boyfriends and why Tata hadn't had one yet. Ace laughed at the pin-ups of the cover boy Gunawan, cut out from magazines by Tata and taped to the side of the wardrobe facing the bed. Gunawan's large eyes gazed deep into their hearts, his thick eyebrows were like lush trees that gave them shade on the hottest day. In one picture, he was brushing aside his shining hair; in another, he was facing down and glancing at them mysteriously. In yet another, he was pouting his full, wet lips – with baggy jeans hanging around his hips, his hands playing with the fine hairs around his navel.

'Ta, if your type is Tiko, you will never find a boyfriend at school.' Tata flinched at the word Tiko, an offensive term for 'native' Indonesians that her family forbade her to use.

But she didn't say anything, only pinched Ace's stomach, making her wince.

'I can't help it, Ce.'

'At our age, we don't have to kiss only the people we like. Do it for experience's sake. To know what it feels like.'

'How does it feel?'

'Kissing?'

'Have you done anything else?'

Ace snorted as if Tata didn't deserve to know the answer. She looked at the ceiling that was peeling away here and there.

'Kissing is everything. Our lips are one of the most sensitive parts of our body. Before your first kiss, you only used them for yourself, for talking and eating. But when your lips meet another person's, they cause friction that sparks electricity in every part of your body. It turns off the mind and turns on all the other parts – they light up, they explode, while your brain is resting, not thinking at all. That's when I feel most alive, when I'm not thinking.' Ace smiled mischievously. 'Do you want to practice with me?'

'Don't be crazy, Ce!' Tata blushed, even as she jokingly hit Ace on the head.

'What did I just say? You don't have to have a crush on the person you're kissing. Think of it as a science experiment. Who knows, maybe there's no difference between a boy's lips and a girl's? The school's mathlete can't be rational all of a sudden? Just feel what's on your lips, not what's in here,' she pointed to her chest while barely holding in her laughter.

Tata grabbed a pillow and pressed it to Ace's face. It was hard for Tata not to admire the madness of her friend – someone who was so comfortable with herself, her thoughts and feelings, wherever she was, as if her happiness didn't depend on anyone else, as if no one could touch her, no one could hurt her.

Tata had a face that many people say is sweet, meaning it was pleasing to the eye because it was not threatening or envy-inducing. Some boys at school actually paid attention to her, asked her about homework, walked with her to the cafeteria, and even gave her Valentine cards. Several times those boys also asked her out to Dunkin' Donuts or Dairy Queen after school. Tata knew her parents wouldn't mind, and she could afford those places on her allowance – but she always turned down their invitations with the excuse of having to help her mother at the store.

In addition to running the shop, her father had a side job with his friend in Glodok who traded in luxury car parts. He dreamed of taking his wife to Taiwan one day. If Tata was selected to represent their school, she would be competing in the Science Olympics there. Tata and her family had never been abroad.

Tata's parents never asked her if she had any boyfriends. Perhaps it was clear to them that she didn't, because no boy had ever visited her at home. They weren't worried. The pictures of Gunawan in Tata's room were quite a relief for them, although they'd be happier if they had been pictures of Andy Lau or Aaron Kwok, which adorned the room of Wiwin, the family's housemaid. They knew of Gunawan from a soap opera, but never expected Tata to nickname her bolster pillow Gugu and treat it as Gunawan himself. She used the pillow whenever her body needed release or her brain needed comforting from whatever problem was bothering her. Even though Gugu had been a comfort so far, Tata never stopped imagining the real thing. If, for every action there was an equal and opposite reaction, then what Ace said had to be true: two pairs of lips must contain protons and electrons that pushed and pulled one another to create energy bursts that would wake up every nerve in the two lovers' bodies.

During recess, Ace waited impatiently for Tata to leave her classroom. 'Come to my house this Saturday, OK? We'll watch *Buffy, the Vampire Slayer*. It's a new American show. We'll go to my house directly from school, so don't forget to tell your mum and dad. Pak Seno will drive you home.'

Tata was surprised and excited. She remembered what her father had said about the sun setting in the north in Jakarta, not in the west. She really wanted to see that fabulous view.

'We have a satellite dish, so my brother and I can record good shows from abroad. He has a VHS player that can be timed to record any show we want. You haven't met him yet, have you? His name is Tian, short for Sebastian. Fair warning, Ta, he looks a lot like Gunawan. His friends call him Tian Tiko,' Ace laughed.

Tata didn't laugh. She couldn't figure out why anyone would think that nickname was funny. Mentioning someone's ethnicity, even in a joking and friendly manner, made her uncomfortable. Imagine if someone called her Tata Cokin, just because she was ethnically Chinese? She winced. *Better to be called Cina or Tionghoa or even Amoy*, she thought. But Tata wondered if she was being too serious. After all, it was Ace, her good friend, who always took things lightly without ever thinking about the consequences.

Her discomfort quickly dissolved into curiosity about Tian. *How similar is he to Gunawan? Is Ace just teasing her?* Tata couldn't wait until Saturday. Usually, she was content with watching *Friends* or *Beverly Hills 90210* on RCTI as her weekend entertainment. Now both seemed lame compared to the story of a teenage vampire-killer, and the chance to visit her best friend's house for the first time and meet a boy who looked like Gunawan.

Tata usually wouldn't venture north except to eat fresh seafood at roadside stalls in Muara Karang or for recreation at Ancol park. This time with Ace, in her quiet car, Tata went all the way to the northernmost point of Jakarta. The car drove through Angke's chaos, and Jembatan Tiga – which was crammed full of shophouses and malls – and entered the Pluit area, marked by the Heaven Funeral Home. The small houses soon gave way to large houses, like those in *Beverly Hills 90210*. Tata noticed she was feeling lighter than usual on this car ride; her heart didn't race like when she was on the bus or in her father's old Kijang. In Ace's car, she couldn't hear the clashing of old and new civilisations outside. Like a silent war movie, this vehicle seemed to numb her. The further north they went, the more Tata saw blue. Even the sky seemed bluer. With nothing blocking her view, all the way to the horizon, it felt even easier to breathe.

Is this the furthest corner of this city, out of reach of most people and even the developers? It seemed that the homeowners up here couldn't be pressured or coerced to move in any way.

Ace's house was huge like a white castle with towering pillars. Tata followed her inside and up the winding stairs to the living room. There stood a young man, wearing shorts and a *Poltergeist* T-shirt.

'Hi, Tiko,' said Ace.

'Hi, Cokin,' Tian replied.

Tata flushed extra red. Not only because of the greetings that the brother and sister exchanged, but also because of how much Tian looked like Gunawan. Ace was not making it up. Tian had super thick eyebrows, big melancholic eyes, a sharp nose, full lips, and clean brown skin. He also wore glasses. The only difference was Tian was shorter.

'Ta, this is Tian, the brother that I love to hate. It's just the two of us. All the good looks from our parents went to him. But I got all the brains, haha!'

Tian laughed somewhat reluctantly and welcomed Tata's extended hand with a faint smile. 'Hi.'

He set the VHS playing and left the room. Even though Tian only said one word to her, it already made Tata very happy. Tian was exactly like Gunawan – handsome, calm, and distant.

Every Saturday afternoon after school, Tata and Ace watched *Buffy* in Pantai Mutiara. For Tata, Buffy was far cooler than all the girls in Beverly Hills or Central Perk. 'In every generation, there is a chosen one,' said the narrator at the beginning of each episode. 'She alone will stand against the vampires and the demons and the forces of darkness. She is the slayer.'

On every visit, Tian always set up the VHS for them, then left. This caught Tata's interest. There was no way Ace couldn't set it up herself. Tata was sure even she could do it after paying attention a few times. One day Ace joked, 'Come on, Ta, forget Gunawan, why don't you go for Tian? He's more than just a picture on your wardrobe?' Typical Ace. Tata was never sure if Ace knew how her words affected other people, or if she was just kidding. Tata wondered if Ace was trying to tell her that Tian was interested in her, if Ace was encouraging them to get together. But Tata hadn't been raised to dream about things that were beyond her reach or means. So Tata just punched Ace's arm.

Preparing for the 1998 International Science Olympics, taking place in a few months, proved to be draining for Tata and Ace. Both of them knew that Tata had a better chance to be selected to represent their school – Tata was more ambitious, and she worked harder. Tata needed this opportunity more than Ace, but sometimes it upset her that Ace seemed to be letting her win. Or perhaps Ace simply preferred dating to studying. Either way, both agreed that life would be more fun if they had been blessed with supernatural powers rather than brilliant brains. Buffy was always behind in school, but it was no problem for her as she was too busy killing vampires and falling in love. How exciting.

At the end of the second week of May, there was a long weekend, since Vesak Day was on the following Monday. Tata and Ace couldn't wait to watch Buffy's next adventure on the Saturday. By this point, Tian was occasionally joining them to watch the show, but usually just at the end. It was the same that Saturday. He made small talk with Tata, offering her something to drink or asking about her preparation for the Science Olympics. In the middle of the show, Ace complained of having a headache. She went to rest in her bedroom. Without Ace, Tata felt the vibe shifting in the living room. She couldn't ignore the presence of Tian, who was sitting opposite her and concentrating on *Buffy*. Tian absorbed all the energy in the room. Tata felt nervous and changed her sitting position several times.

'Are you bored? Want me to show you my film collection?' said Tian.

Without thinking, Tata followed Tian to his bedroom, with a window overlooking the pier. The splendour of the sea was like a feast for Tata's hungry eyes. She devoured the view out across the Java Sea all the way to the Thousand Islands. Tata saw luxury motorboats moored, reflecting the glow of the evening sun. Tian's face was very close to hers, and it looked even more handsome than ever. He took off his glasses. His eyes sucked

Tata's entire attention. Tian said he hated *Buffy*, and he had much better shows recorded. He told her about his ambition to go to film school, but his parents wouldn't let him. He thought Ace was more suitable to continue the family business. He really admired smart girls like Tata. As soon as his lips touched hers, Tata felt her entire body became the sea. Vast, deep, and rolling with waves. Outside the window, the sun was burning red, slowly descending into the embracing, refreshing sea. Tata didn't get to see the glorious sunset that her father had often mentioned, but she had no regrets.

On Tuesday 12 May, 1998, it was quiet at Tata and Ace's school. The final year students were busy taking the national exams. Ace didn't say much that day. Tata took it to mean that Tian hadn't told his sister about the kiss, and she was relieved. Ace looked a little pale, as if she was still ill. During lessons, Tata tried hard to brush Tian out of her head in vain. Her brain was one big screen replaying the kiss over and over. At about noon, the school made a sudden announcement telling everyone that there was a student demonstration at Trisakti University, not far from there; in case the demonstration turned violent, all students were advised to go home and to avoid areas near the university. Ace hurriedly looked for Tata and drove her home. This time she didn't come in, just asked for a bag of milk candy.

'Until tomorrow, Ce, get plenty of rest.'

'OK, Ta. Tell your dad thank you for the candy and send my regards to your mum.'

Neither of them knew that it was the last day they would ever see each other.

That afternoon it rained heavily; several students were shot by the security forces. Tata's father told his wife and Wiwin to quickly close up the shop. Tata felt nervous seeing thousands of people on the streets calling for President Suharto to step down, the only president she'd ever known. She gathered with her parents and Wiwin in front of the TV, eating their dinner in silence. Tata and her father watched the news about the attacks on the students until after midnight. Her father wondered if there would be demonstrations the following day as well; Tata wondered if Tian was thinking about her.

The next day, and two days later, news of arson and looting gripped Tata's family with fear. On the news, they watched a mob of people torching refuse trucks and petrol stations in Grogol and dozens of cars at Trisakti University and Tarumanegara. The fires spread to several areas in the west and the north. They looted shopping centres and broke into Chinese people's houses and shops. Iie Lani, Tata's auntie, said on the phone that Chinese women had been tortured and raped in the riots. Tata's mother cried in terror.

On TV, Tata watched people running in despair from the savages who were setting malls and shops on fire – the horror on the victims' faces and the cruelty on the perpetrators'. Her whole body was sweating ice. She imagined being trapped in that fire, and was certain she would melt until nothing was left. Tata could still hear Iie Lani hysterically telling her mother to lock all the doors and choose suicide rather than be touched by those evil men.

Tata wept in her father's arms. Her now mature body could relate to the pleasures of being loved and the horrific pain of being violated. What if those demons broke into their house? Smart Renata, now helpless to protect herself and the people she loved. She recalled Buffy. If only she were the chosen one, then she could battle the darkness and defeat it. *Is Ace thinking about the same thing? Is Tian worried about me?* Tata felt very selfish.

Wiwin and her mother somehow kept their wits about them. Wiwin went out and put up the sign *'OWNED BY*

NATIVE INDONESIANS' over the one reading *'SOEN JAYA SHOP'*. Then Tata's mother did something that would forever haunt Tata's memories about the May '98 tragedy: she opened the chicken coop, loaded the chicks and chickens into laundry baskets, and released them onto the streets. Like sacrificial animals. Four basketfuls. Tata heard the shrieks of the chickens running around in a panic, wishing they could fly. Her tears overflowed as she pictured the little chicks, separated from their mothers and trampled by the rioting mass.

Tata called Ace's house several times, but there was no answer. Pantai Mutiara was not mentioned on the news, but Tata was still going mad with worry because there'd been no call from Ace. Tian also consumed her thoughts. After President Suharto announced his resignation, the riots subsided. Tata could not stand it anymore, being cooped up for days inside the house. She wanted to make sure Ace and Tian were OK. On TV, many people had returned to their daily lives. The heart of the city was still beating, even though its body had been paralysed.

'Papa, please take me to Ace's house.'

Tata's father was curious to see the nearby Gajah Mada and Hayam Wuruk districts, which had been completely looted and wrecked. His friend's car parts shop was also looted. Luckily, he survived. Tata's father pulled out his motorbike.

They passed Hayam Wuruk, Glodok, Pinangsia, Old Town, and went along the Krukut River all the way to Pluit. Everything looked as unreal as a movie set: a plundered city. Vampires, demons, and evil spirits had just gorged themselves and left. Shattered citizens were picking up those remnants of their lives that could still be saved. Tata hugged her father's waist even tighter. What was the untold cost of forcing down a dictator? Tata paid for it with a fear that would stay with her for the rest of her life.

After they passed the Heaven Funeral Home, Tata felt she was leaving the movie set and returning to the real world, which was not torn apart at all, just very quiet. Especially when they arrived at Pantai Mutiara. The sea was silent. Tata's father stopped his motorbike in front of the guard's post at Ace's house. Tata had never seen this security guard before. He observed Tata and her father. On an ordinary day, Tata was sure that the guard would think her father was an electronics or car repairman.

'Good afternoon, sir. Is Grace or Ace home?' said Tata. 'I'm Renata, her friend from school, and this is my father.'

The security guard's eyes narrowed. 'Everyone has gone away.'

Tata was stunned. 'Gone away? Where to?'

'None of your business.' The guard raised his voice. 'Now get lost!'

'I'm sorry, sir, my daughter was just —' Tata's father tried to explain, but Tata pulled him away by the hand.

The guard was approaching them. Tata and her father decided to leave.

Tata's father rode his bike as fast as he could, with his daughter's head leaning heavily on his back. He felt his shirt getting wet. When he slowed down, he could hear her crying. He stopped his bike in front of an empty field.

'Tata?'

Tata sobbed in silence.

Her father released her hold on his waist and got off the motorbike. It broke his heart to see Tata so upset. Calling up all his strength, he cupped Tata's face, 'You know, I would have taken you and your mother abroad too, if only we had enough money.'

Tata felt terrible that she had made her father feel poor and helpless. She wanted to say that that wasn't what was bothering her, but she couldn't speak. She was a chicken, and Ace was a bird. When shots had been fired, even though they were best friends, their survival instincts were completely different. In the end, someone left and the other was left behind. Tata did not blame Ace for leaving, but she couldn't help but feel abandoned. When the country was in turmoil, people like Tata's family became shields for people like Ace's family. Her family was lucky – this time. It made Tata think of the chickens that her mother had released, in exchange for their lives.

Tata's father wasn't to know that there could be someone out there who could make his daughter feel so small and cast aside. If only he knew, at some point in a teenage girls' life, the hands that touched her body could be more paralysing than those that won her heart.

Later that year, Tata represented her school at the Science Olympics in Taipei, though she didn't bring home any medals. Still, several well-known universities offered her a scholarship. At the end of the year, she received an email from Ace. Her family had settled in Oregon in the States. Ace apologised for not writing to Tata until then. She also said that she was being treated for the headache that never went away. She asked if Tata had a boyfriend. Not once did she mention the May tragedy, as if it never happened. Tata couldn't help feeling betrayed. Her best friend had left her, looking for safety, without saying a word, while she was trapped, scared to death and continually worrying about her. Now Tata knew why Ace was always so confident and comfortable in herself. She was immune from tragedy and the consequences of her actions. She was a free, flying being, unable to put herself in another's shoes. Tata stopped admiring her. She did not reply to the email.

Twenty years later.

Google. The Twin Towers. The invasion of Iraq. The tsunami in Aceh. Facebook. Snow in the Middle East. The economic crisis. Gus Dur being impeached. The first female president of Indonesia. The Bali Bombing. SARS. 4G. Global warming. The first Christian, ethnically Chinese governor of Jakarta. Fundamentalism. Trump. Racism. The world was progressing, and regressing, growing more connected and separated at the same time. People changed and lost direction.

One day, Tian knocked on Tata's door. She lived not far from her childhood home and was taking care of her sick father. Tian had gained weight, but was still handsome. His mannerisms were colder. Tata shuddered at the sight of him. She no longer had any illusions about him. Tian had become a stranger to her. He came with news of Ace's death from a brain tumour. Her last wish was to have Tata join the family to spread her ashes in Pantai Mutiara at sunset. Ace wanted to spend eternity in the sea where her mother was also laid to rest. She wanted to be eulogised by those closest to her in that beautiful place. Tata was quiet for a while, looking for grief or sorrow in her heart. All she found was a scar, which no longer pained her but reminded her that people were born differently, had different preferences and carried different shaped wounds. *Know your place, know yourself* – that was Tata's family's principle, which had helped her avoid many disappointments and kept her from dreaming of the impossible. Tata regretted that Ace's brilliant life had to end at such a young age, even though she knew nothing about her life in the States. Still, she felt no grief or sorrow. She remembered Ace's kindness, but was it wrong if now she only considered Ace a former high school friend? Their teenage years together meant little more to her than the old books and drawings that she had given away. Twenty years was a long time to cement or erase memories. Tata had learned how to move on, to forget events and people in order to keep going.

Even though her heart wasn't moved, Tata was touched that Ace still considered her a close friend. But she was sure she wouldn't be able to hold Ace's ashes. It was a flattering but burdensome request. Ashes are sacred. Tata felt she had no right, and that it wasn't her duty. So she said to Tian, 'I'll have to see how my father is doing that day.' Tata sensed Tian understood her reluctance. Through the iron bars, Tata watched Tian walk away, away from the houses that once had terraces and garages that opened out onto the streets, now barricaded with sturdy fences. The neighbourhood felt more cramped that way, but was safer. Still uncertain about how to answer this call of the past that had come suddenly, Tata promised to Ace that one day, when she was ready, she would come visit her at Pantai Mutiara, and, finally, watch the sun set in the north.

All Theatre is False

Afrizal Malna

Translated by Syarafina Vidyadhana

HE HAD A LARGE frame. Sturdy. People would walk past him and think he could be an actor. He *was* an actor, but first and foremost, he was a person. The kind that would almost always leave his long sleeves unbuttoned. The kind you could almost always find near the Taman Ismail Marzuki[1] complex in Cikini, where artists from all over Jakarta often hung out. Very few people knew where he came from – some said he was from Sumbawa. He had the kind of stare that was so intense you could almost see his eyes glisten. Although no one knew for certain what it was he was staring at.

Standing in front of the wall of Taman Ismail Marzuki, he looked as if he were facing a Master who no longer presented in human form. He stared at the wall. Flat. A flat surface had always tempted him to… he wasn't sure what. An actor could only live and walk in their own body.

Having never trodden a single stage or performed a single show, one might question whether he truly was an actor. But then again, wasn't the whole world a stage and all of us merely players? Putting on a show for as long as we are alive. Or for as long as we believe ourselves to be.

'I cannot exist every day. Some days I need to also not exist,' he said coldly to the wall. He reached deep into his trouser pocket and took out a few cigarette butts that he'd collected from the streets – the only explanation as to how his trousers smelled more like an ashtray than his own mouth. He picked one brand that he liked best: Mascot. He lit the cigarette, what was left of it anyway, and took a nice long drag. The smoke penetrated his lungs and filled them up. As he took his last puff, he could taste the breath of the person who last smoked it. It was almost two in the afternoon. He wasn't hungry yet. Or maybe he was just used to the feeling.

'Frans!' someone called out to him. It could have been anyone – another artist from the neighbourhood – but Frans didn't budge.

'Ooh… look at him go.'

'*Beep boop…* Frans is not available at the moment!' said another voice, amused. Frans kept walking. It was as if the whole world was flat today. Nothing else existed but himself. Or, maybe, today he was also flat and therefore nothing was here at all. He wasn't going to push, and he certainly didn't want to be pushed. Today he felt like taking a break from personhood. Which also meant taking a break from hunger and other appetites. The only exceptions, he decided, were for smoking and walking.

He knew the neighbourhood like the back of his hand. Every day he would walk from one building to the next; from Teater Terbuka to Wisma Seni, from Studio Huriah Adam to Kantin Roro Mendut, from Teater Tertutup to Teater Arena, then all the way to Galeri Cipta (which is sadly no more). Every day he would walk around these buildings like an animal roaming outside of its cage for the first time. This was his home, his country, his native land – all within this small complex. In his mind, Indonesia did not exist for there was only Taman Ismail Marzuki. But no one there recognised him as the artist that he was, because he had never created anything that the industry deemed as art.

The cigarette butt he was smoking had run out of tobacco to keep it burning. The flame spread and singed the filter, letting out a sharp, tangy smell before finally going out. Frans squatted down as he started to dig a hole with his hands, his fingernails kept long on each. He put the cigarette butt inside the hole and buried it. Then he rose up – proud, like he had just ticked something off his daily checklist.

'Frans, what are you doing?' said a familiar voice, a female actor from Teater Kecil who was passing by. Frans didn't say anything back. He was on leave – which part of this did they not understand. Today he was not a person. He wanted to tell her that he was hungry, but he had learned that the hunger felt by one person may not be the same as another. No matter how loud it screamed.

'I haven't fucked in two months,' Frans said instead. The female actor, who would play Euis in the upcoming show, *A Bottomless Well: A Play in Four Acts* by Arifin C. Noer, was clearly taken aback. She stopped walking at once and looked at him: should she be offended? Seeing her reaction, Frans, ever so casually, began unzipping his trousers. But before they were completely down, the woman was out of sight.

Frans turned around to face the wall, and spat on it.

'You see that? For an actor, she sure is anti-theatre. Anti-performance. Where's the actor? Where's the theatre? The performance remains buried alive inside my trousers!' Frans shouted at the wall. 'How easy it is to live as a man, as an asshole,' he murmured. 'And even easier to assume what women want.' Frans then spat on his own hand and walked away. He knew not why or where he must walk. He knew only that he had to. To experience each and every space like it was his little corner of the world. Walking, he felt, had nothing to do with distance and everything to do with the event of walking itself.

At night, Frans would sleep in front of a closed shop, any closed shop around Cikini, or in the back of a cheap hotel in Gondangdia, not too far from Taman Ismail Marzuki. Sometimes he would sleep next to Jijok, his friend who, much like himself, was a performance artist and lived on the street.

The security guards at Taman Ismail Marzuki did not see them as artists, but rather a couple of petty thieves. That's because every time they were around, something somewhere always went missing. Nonetheless, Frans and Jijok considered themselves regulars; whether it was a theatrical, dance, or music performance, they would always find a way to sneak into the building. But they were never there for the art. Instead, they would sleep for the full duration of the show. They saw it as a chance, if not the only chance, to sleep in a proper setting – in soft and comfortable seats, no less.

Ali Sadikin, the Jakarta Governor at the time, who was also a regular, didn't recognise their artistry either. To him Frans and Jijok were nothing more than a couple of homeless bums.

'Like I give a shit,' Frans would say. 'They can call me whatever they like: a bum, a thief, an artist. Living on the street is just one of the many ways to live!' he would add, with pride, to anyone who made fun of him. Frans always took it seriously even when he knew they were probably only messing with him.

An object could leave a mark, and possibly shape its own narrative, if it was placed in a space strong enough to sustain it. Then it would become indomitable. This was why Frans insisted on maintaining his qualities. A task he deemed equivalent to that of keeping a chocolate bar from melting under the sun. Because once it melted, the shape would be irreversibly damaged – even if it tasted all the same.

Frans put his index finger on his forehead, mimicking a handgun. He said, quite convincingly, 'Bang! This brain, as you well know, is not made of books, but of dust from the streets. Thinking on the street is not the same as thinking from inside your bedroom!' People around him burst out laughing. Marus, a parking attendee with a stab wound on his face, walked over to him and offered him a cigarette.

'Oh, thank you, my friend,' Frans took one cigarette and lit it right away. He inhaled it deep, his lungs welcoming its smoky embrace.

'Intellectualism is not a museum but the shit that dries up under the sun!' Frans continued his lecture as he exhaled the smoke through his nose. His stare remained intense. People around him started laughing again.

'All it took was one cigarette for you to spew philosophical bullshit,' one of them sneered. 'What would happen if we gave you a pack, eh? I bet Philosophy itself would get sick with all that smoke.'

'But you're wrong!' Frans threw his cigarette on the ground and stubbed it out.

'You see, I live under the sun. Not inside a pack of cigarettes. Now tell me, what can't grow under the sun? You've all become stupid because you traded the sun for neon lights,' he said as he was walking away. As if suddenly he was reminded of something important he had to do. His sleeves were fluttering in the wind. His long hair was fluttering, too – you could see the sun peeking between the strands.

★

Jijok sat at the back of the audience, barefoot and cross-legged on a floor mat inside the Huriah Adam building where a discussion of a recently released film was taking place. Every time they had a film discussion, the people in the audience looked quite different from the usual types. Nicer. That's because most of them were artists working in film, and as such they always looked more stylish, more presentable than those who didn't work in film – especially compared to the performance artists, like Frans and Jijok, who were notorious for looking like they'd never heard of soap powder. Jijok was listening to the talk when his eyes caught Frans circling the building through the windows. When Frans finally came inside, he just stood at the back, reluctant to sit down with the rest of the audience. Dozens of pairs of shoes were lined up by the entrance.

'It's a film discussion… come sit next to me,' Jijok whispered to Frans.

'No. This is bullshit! This is money-speak!' Frans exclaimed. The whole room was staring, but he didn't care. He stared back at every single one of them before stepping outside. When the discussion ended not long after, people stood up from the floor and tried to find their shoes. Among the crowd, one particular young director looked lost. It appeared that he could not find his shoes. Seeing the look on his face, Jijok grew wary. *This could turn ugly fast.*

The security guard looked ashamed as he started to realise what was happening. An up-and-coming director had lost his shoes on his watch. He knew exactly what he had to do, and so immediately looked for Frans.

Frans was sitting by the fish pond at the intersection of Teater Tertutup, Teater Arena, and Huriah Adam. He appeared calm. The security guard spotted his signature long trousers, rolled up to above his calves. On his feet were a pair of clean, brand new shoes.

The young director soon joined them at the fish pond and told the security guard that they were, in fact, his shoes on Frans' feet.

'You embarrassed me, Frans. Not only did you steal his shoes, you had the nerve to flaunt them like this!' The security guard was on the verge of losing his temper.

'What do you mean, "stole"?' Frans stood up as if to give them all a better look at the shoes. Several people began to gather around Frans, the security guard, and the young director who was standing barefoot.

'Look at these shoes — *look!* These shoes look so much better on me than on him,' Frans pointed at the young director. 'So wouldn't you think, since I wear them better, that they *must* be mine?'

The crowd was stunned at the absurdity.

'You fucking lunatic!'

Frans walked away as soon as he heard the word 'lunatic'. He left like nothing had happened, like it was not in any way a delicate situation.

'Thief!' The security guard shouted at Frans. But before he started after him, the young director stopped him.

'It's OK, I don't mind,' the young director said. 'Those shoes look better on him anyway, so he should keep them. After all, I believe in the importance of aesthetics.'

Jijok separated himself from the crowd and went after Frans. 'You crossed the line, Frans. Why did you do that? You could've gotten beaten up, or worse.'

'Don't. You've been brainwashed. Do you know what Truth is? You can't possibly understand the truth if you trouble yourself with false morality. You're just like them, you have no idea how philosophy is practised on the street,' Frans sounded disappointed. 'Now you're only beginning to recognise the Truth, in all its glory, as it stands tall in front of you, in a brand new pair of shoes. There's no doubt about it, like the certainty of that Descartes you idolise so much. We're on the street, not inside a house, an art studio, or the governor's office. We don't hold any positions of power. All there is is dust. So might as well enjoy it. No point in complaining...'

Jijok spotted two long cigarette butts near his feet and picked them up. He gave one to Frans. They lit them and took a drag. It was nice, as if their bodies were clouds floating in the sun rays.

'So truth equals stolen shoes, eh?' Jijok tried to carry on the conversation.

'Cool, right? Look at my feet!' Frans jumped up and down, dancing in his new shoes. Jijok was amused. Impressed. Immersed. To Jijok, Frans' little performance epitomised what it was to be human. A soul that should answer only to itself; a body that should move only according to its own will, untroubled by entrances and exits; a mind capable of seeing treasure in a pile of trash. Everything was something. There wouldn't be two of the same thing. And this could only happen once.

★

The sun had long set. Frans and Jijok finished scouting the streets for bits of cardboard to sleep on in front of a bakery in Cikini. As they tried to close their eyes, it dawned on them what little sleep could do to salvage the night. The residual smell of baked goods filled the air. That, and the smell of petrol fumes and sewage from under the sidewalks. Their stomachs growled. Their hunger became more unendurable by the minute.

'Have you got some money, Frans?' Jijok broke the silence.

'Money? What for?'

'I'm starving!'

'Me too.'

'Ugh, why did you even ask *what for*. You got my hopes up for a second there.'

'Well, it is hope that got us starving in the first place. Now knock it off. Don't act like some spoiled artist or philosopher. Hunger *is* an integral part of a living, material body.'

'You know what, Frans,' Jijok raised his voice. 'I've had it up to here with you. You're so full of shit. Hunger means *hunger*. Stop romanticising it. Would you rather I kill myself tonight just so I can prove there is nothing philosophical or poetic about starving?'

Frans didn't say another word that night.

★

The street in front of the bakery was slowly getting busy. As the sun rose higher, cars, motorbikes, and city buses began to fill the street. It was around this time that the two of them would get up to leave before the shop owners came and kicked them out. But when Jijok opened his eyes, Frans was nowhere to be seen. He got up, collected the cardboard, and put it in the bin. With sleepy eyes, Jijok then walked toward Taman Ismail Marzuki, to Teater Arena to be exact, where he planned on resuming his sleep. He had about three hours before the security guard would show up and tell him to leave. And so there he was, lying on his back, against the cold floor of a theatre building.

Jijok couldn't tell how long he'd been asleep for when Frans came towards him, carrying two nasi bungkus.

'Eat,' Frans said to Jijok as he handed one of them to him.

'So you lied to me last night, Frans? You did have money, huh?' Jijok sneered.

'Look at my feet! Yeah, I'm back in my old shoes. Went to see the ragman earlier and sold those shiny shoes,' Frans said. 'Now we can eat.'

'Thank you, Frans,' Jijok said with a full mouth. Tempe goreng. Tahu sayur. Sambal. Kerupuk. Teh manis panas. Later in the morning, Jijok had to go to the youth centre to prepare for a show that he was directing. His theatre collective had just won a prize at the annual Youth Theatre Festival held in five youth centres across Jakarta. As the winner, they now had the privilege of performing on a more prestigious stage: Taman Ismail Marzuki.

★

The show was about to begin. This would be the first time for Jijok's theatre collective to perform in the Teater Arena at Taman Ismail Marzuki. Jijok cleaned up nice, he even took a shower and put on his best clothes. After sharing his final notes with the actors and the stage manager, Jijok left the stage. *Tonight the general public will finally see me as a theatre director*, he told himself. He decided it would be better for him to watch the show from the stalls, and so he left the backstage area to go and queue in front of the entrance.

But as he was about to step in through the doors, the security guard stopped him.

'I can't let you come inside.'

'Are you serious? I'm the director!'

'A thief is what you are! And thieves don't get to come inside,' the guard said. 'Besides, you look nothing like a director.'

Jijok didn't know what to do. He couldn't convince the guy that he was really a director – *the* director. In the end, he had to wait outside for the full duration of the play. He didn't get to see the fruits of his own labour.

★

Frans and Jijok were lying on their backs outside one of the shops downtown. This time it was a bike shop, to avoid the smell of bread that almost pushed them over the edge last time.

'I can't even watch my own play, Frans,' Jijok sighed.

'What did I tell you? All theatre is false. And every show at TIM is fake theatre. The real theatre is here. On these bits of cardboard. In front of this shop. On the street. Among the dust… where we try to escape from the smell of bread.'

'Frans…' Jijok said quietly. 'To be honest, I don't even know what theatre is.'

'Honesty is good. That's something that lot never have. They act like they know so much about theatre, when they don't even have what it takes to confront the truth. All this time I've been acting like a madman just to please them. They wanted me to appear like a madman, and so I appeared like a madman. I did it all so they could understand what humanity, madness, and theatre mean. But as you can see, I'm not mad! Only you can see me for what I am. Nobody else. They would rather believe I'm a lunatic,' Frans told Jijok. 'So, yeah, I think you know better than anyone what theatre means. I mean, what even is the "people's theatre"? Those people are nothing but a bunch of bourgeoisies who despise the poor. Being poor…'

'Please. I'm not hungry tonight,' Jijok cut him off. 'So I don't need your lecture. I'm just tired.'

Jijok hugged himself and murmured, 'I'm so tired.'

Frans sat up and began massaging Jijok's foot. As Jijok started to feel more relaxed, he could see his life flashing before his eyes like a fast-changing montage. Each memory seemed to make its own music. They collided and intersected with one another, like a saw that kept sawing to make the teeth grow sharper each time. Deeper. They took him further and further into an endless tunnel of dreams. Frans knew his friend had fallen asleep from the sound of his breathing – steady, much steadier than when he was awake.

Nevertheless, Frans kept massaging Jijok's body. 'Now it's time I apologise to myself, for treating myself like a madman for so long,' Frans whispered to his friend. He stared at the street with a thrill.

Jijok was sound asleep under the Jakartan sky. Frans rose from the ground and left Jijok where he was. From that day on, no one ever saw Frans anymore. He had gone. Vanished. Like everything else that had passed.

Note

1. Taman Ismail Marzuki, popularly known as TIM, is an arts, cultural, and science centre in Cikini, Jakarta. The complex comprises a number of facilities including six performing arts theaters, cinemas, exhibition hall, gallery, libraries and an archive building. TIM is named after Ismail Marzuki, one of Indonesia's most influential composers.

A Day in the Life of a Guy from Depok who Travels to Jakarta

Yusi Avianto Pareanom

Translated by Daniel Owen

HE LIVED IN DEPOK, West Java. Or let's just say the suburbs of Jakarta, it's easier that way. Though he wasn't crazy about the city he lived in, he was always reluctant to leave if he didn't really have to. Actually, since he had made the decision to work from home a few years ago, he'd been able to stay in the house for days on end. And so, if he absolutely had to go to Jakarta to take care of something or other, he'd often try to accomplish however many other errands on the same day so as not to waste time. This is the story of one of those days.

At ten in the morning, he was on the commuter train from Depok Station to Jakarta. The train wasn't totally packed, but dozens of people still had to stand, including him. At Pondok Cina Station, a woman around fifty years old got on. She looked around for an empty seat, but, of course, there weren't any. A train conductor in uniform with a boyish face moved towards her, taking it upon himself to wake a sleeping passenger: a tall, brawny youth with a slightly bedraggled look. The conductor smacked him brusquely on the shoulder a few times until the youth, who must have been in quite a

111

deep sleep, woke with a start and offered his seat to the woman, who wore a headscarf. But the youth didn't stop there. Grabbing the conductor's hand, he asked why he'd chosen him. It wasn't as if he was sitting in a priority seat – there was actually some other kid sitting nearby, also a young guy, and he wasn't getting kicked out of his seat. The guy from Depok who was going to Jakarta was pleased to see the young man stand up to the conductor, who suddenly seemed perplexed. He suspected the young man was being stereotyped as one of those 'heroic' outdoorsy types; someone who shouldn't fall asleep on the train. A few other passengers joined in, offering their opinions on the situation. The expression on the conductor's boyish face became more and more miserable with each station they passed. The woman in the headscarf sat calmly enough, but the look on her face betrayed her discomfort. The guy from Depok listened attentively as they discussed rights, common decency, and so on. But he had to get off at Gondangdia Station, losing the chance to find out how the conversation, which had captivated his interest, turned out.

The guy from Depok walked from Gondangdia Station to the US Embassy. He had an appointment that day with a consular employee to be interviewed for his visa application. Once inside, he joined the queue in front of the entrance counter. A young woman in a headscarf stood in front of him. She looked like a college student. Greeting him in English, she invited him to take her place because she was waiting for a friend who was still filling out a form. He thanked her, in Indonesian, and continued to wait in line.

At the counter, our man from Depok removed the paperwork from his backpack. Ten seconds later, he winced all of a sudden and apologised. He'd left behind the most important document, his passport. He was astonished by his own idiocy. The night before, he'd placed his passport on his desk and must have forgotten to put it in his bag before leaving. He blamed himself, having barely slept a wink that night. He had a bad habit of not being able to sleep when he had an appointment the next day. He apologised profusely once again to the consular employee, who apparently found his negligence endearing, saying that it wasn't a big deal, he could follow up with the passport the next day.

He was grateful, but nevertheless cursed silently to himself because it meant he'd have to come back again for the exact same errand. His new passport had already proven itself to be unwilling to cooperate. A few weeks earlier, the clerk at the Depok immigration office had needed to apologise to him because they'd made a mistake in the gender printed on his passport. He was used to having people who had never met him in person call him 'Mbak' or 'Bu'[1] when calling or writing to him for the first time. His first name was unisex. But the incident at the immigration office didn't fail to astound him as the very same immigration clerk had interviewed him and taken his picture, and he'd clearly gone months without shaving in the photo. This incident had been funny enough to make a character in a Sapardi Djoko Damono poem cry with laughter.

The guy from Depok who forgot to bring his passport had another appointment at two that afternoon, in the Kuningan area. He still had about three hours to kill. He considered grabbing a bite, but abandoned the idea once he saw a Transjakarta tour bus in front of the US Embassy. He'd never taken this free ride before. For a lark, he hopped on. The conductor greeted him in Japanese. Amused, he responded in the same language and proceeded to pretend to speak Indonesian with a Japanese accent to impress the conductor. Twenty minutes or so passed on the bus, coasting around the Monas area.

After he'd had enough, he got off and hailed a taxi.

'Good afternoon, Sir,' the taxi driver greeted him.

The guy from Depok smiled. He suspected the driver addressed him as 'Sir' because he assumed he was Korean or Japanese. Responding in Indonesian, he asked the driver to take him to Kuningan, at which the driver seemed pleasantly surprised – probably because he spoke Indonesian, not because he'd asked him to drive to Kuningan. He read the driver's name on the dashboard: Sidratul Muntaha. *Amazing,* he thought. This was the first time he'd ever met someone named after the lote tree that marks the end of the seventh heaven, a boundary no living being can pass.

'What do you go by, Pak?' asked the guy from Depok.

'Habib.'[2]

The guy from Depok who had earlier been mistaken for an East Asian then asked Sidratul Muntaha his age. He asked because he was impressed, the driver looked like he was almost seventy years old, and still seemed full of life. His guess wasn't far from the mark: the driver was 65.

'Amazing, Pak, 65 years old and still driving,' said the guy from Depok.

'I gotta stay out of the house. My old lady's too much,' said Sidratul Muntaha.

The guy from Depok was actually prepared for the standard response. Something like 'if you don't work, your body'll start falling apart' or 'I still have dependents,' things that he was used to hearing whenever he met a taxi driver over 60, to which he'd respond with some praise for their determination to keep working. But he was wrong. The guy from Depok wanted to ask what he meant by 'too much,' but Sidratul Muntaha spoke first.

'What religion are you, Bapak?'

The guy from Depok grimaced. 'Why do you ask, Pak?'

'If you're Muslim, I'll invite you to meet my teacher in

Banten sometime. You look like you've got something going for you, Bapak.' Sidratul Muntaha said.

'What would I have going for me?'

'Ilmu,[3] of course. A supernatural ability. Check it out, if you meet my teacher, whatever it is you got, he can make it even more effective.'

'Effective for what?'

'You could use it to get women if you want.'

The guy from Depok, who hadn't heard the word 'effective' used like this in ages, started to laugh. 'Do I look like I need something going for me to get women, Pak?'

'No, no, that's not what I meant, Pak. It's helpful ilmu, ya know. There's nothing wrong with that.'

The guy from Depok started laughing again. He actually wanted to ask Sidratul Muntaha why he didn't use the ilmu he got from his teacher to make his wife stop being 'too much.' Instead, he asked, 'What exactly are your teacher's spiritual powers?'

'They're not spiritual powers, Pak. It's all borrowed from Allah anyway, ya know. There are lots of examples. Like, say a thief gets into your house, all he has to do is stick his hands on the wall. Just like that, the thief can't move or get out of there again. He's got all kinds of ways.'

'Mashallah, that is amazing. Of all his supernatural abilities, what do you think is most extraordinary?'

'He usually prays on a prayer mat that's placed on top of flowing water.'

The guy from Depok wanted to hear more from Sidratul Muntaha about ilmu and supernatural abilities. Unfortunately, they'd arrived at the Setiabudi Building. His two o'clock appointment wasn't at this exact location, but he needed to get something to eat first.

He chose a Greek restaurant in the Setiabudi Building because it had a smokers' corner. Finishing his lunch of tzatziki and moussaka, he opened his phone to take a look at the latest news. The first headline was about a bombing at a hospital in Quetta, Pakistan: 72 killed and 120 wounded. *A hospital! The ruthlessness of man truly knows no bounds*, the guy from Depok thought. He braced himself so as to not vomit up his lunch, wishing to be back in Sidratul Muntaha's taxi, lulled by his stories.

The two o'clock meeting was short and sweet. The businessman, who'd once hired him to landscape his fruit orchard, wanted to hire him again, this time for his newly-married daughter's house. He had a third appointment after Maghrib prayers. To kill time, he went back to the Setiabudi Building, just a few buildings down from where he had met the businessman.

At first he wanted to go for a coffee and smoke hookah, but, on a whim, he stopped by the cinema, where the film *Suicide Squad* caught his eye. He'd liked Margot Robbie in *The Wolf of Wall Street* and wanted to see her play Harley Quinn. Eleven minutes into the film, he dozed off. An hour or so later, he woke up, spending the rest of the film trying to figure out what was going on.

Next, the guy from Depok who went to Jakarta was meeting five old college friends in Pecenongan. All his friends, besides him, were still working in the world of cartography, his major at the Faculty of Engineering at Gadjah Mada University in Yogyakarta. He'd never even once worked in the field of cartography, despite seven years of study in college. Since high school, his real interest lay in designing gardens and parks. He cringed quietly to himself as his friends got carried away in conversation about mapping projects and the specifications of measuring technology. He'd long accepted that he understood less and less of the world of cartography. This fact depressed him a little, because it brought a certain matter squarely to his attention: he'd never mastered cartography, and most of what he learned at high school was now forgotten. So the heights of his academic prowess levelled off after middle school. *Well, what can you do,* he thought. Nevertheless, he didn't regret his college major because he'd made such good friends on the course.

That night, he and his friends hung out at a tented-over warung that sold coffee, ginger tea, and snacks. Just as they were getting lost in conversation, a young man approached, selling sandals. He reached out as if to shake hands and greeted them the Muslim way. Because the guy from Depok and his friends really didn't need any sandals, they turned down his offer. The young man went on his way, but returned ten minutes or so later, pleading with them to buy some sandals. The guy from Depok who had gone to Jakarta told the young man that he was bothering them and advised him to be more industrious in his effort to make a living. What was to come next the guy from Depok who had long failed to master the skills of cartography would never have imagined. The young man begged their forgiveness by letting out a long, shrill howl, and inviting the guy from Depok to slap him in the face because he'd disturbed their gathering. Slap me as hard as you want, as long as you give me some money, he said.

The guy from Depok had always thought those groups of buskers who would rather humiliate themselves and talk trash about everyone else than actually sing to earn their meagre handfuls of coins were among those who could most efficiently ruin your day. Turns out there was someone even more unnerving.

At 9pm the guy from Depok, our beleaguered hero, was back on the commuter train in the direction of home. He got on at Juanda Station and sat down. As the train began to move, he found himself still disturbed by the young sandal seller's behaviour, which had aggravated him so much in Pecenongan.

Who could have guessed that his exasperation would soon disappear thanks to an unexpected acapella offering. A young guy with bangs was belting out some song without realising where he was. His ear was plugged with an earphone connected to some music player gadget. Maybe because he was truly enraptured, or maybe because he was performing some kind of ritual, his eyes were more closed than open as he sang. The guy from Depok who was now on his way home didn't recognise the songs the youth was crooning. He wasn't even sure if he was singing in a language known to man.

'Oh boy, he has failed the audition,' the young woman sitting next to our beloved man from Depok said.

Another passenger recited the name of Allah over and over, grousing about what the heck this kid thought he was doing. Another passenger pouted at the sound of the young man's voice, without raising the Lord's name. The consensus on the train: this kid was a real, shameless nuisance. The guy from Depok, who suddenly felt his heart lift, didn't share their opinion. He said that this young singer was a real entertainer, and quite talented, because he could sing in so many different keys at once. The rest of the passengers cracked up.

Passing through Cawang Station, the guy from Depok who was now on his way home remembered that there was a folk music performance that night at the Coffeewar coffee shop in Kemang Timur and he'd promised the owner that he'd be there. He got off at Kalibata Station and hopped in a taxi toward Kemang Timur.

After a few minutes of small talk, the taxi driver suggested polygamy for the guy from Depok who didn't go straight home. His name was Amran, he was fifty-five years old, and had eleven kids and two grandchildren. At first, Amran, who sported a lengthy beard, asked his passenger how many children he had. Two, the guy from Depok answered. Amran advised him to have another kid or two, so as to be more prosperous and have the chance to father a truly pious child, who could open the gates of heaven for him. The guy from Depok said that two kids were quite enough, and, for a variety of reasons, he couldn't possibly ask his wife to have another child.

'Well, if that's the case, just find a new vessel, Pak,' Amran said.

Struck by a wave of drowsiness, our man from Depok didn't feel like arguing. But as a result, Amran became increasingly enthusiastic. He went on to explain the population ratio between men and 'vessels,' one to six.

'If you marry again, they'll help take care of them, Pak,' he said. 'In Kampung Melayu alone, right around where I live, there are 400 unmarried ladies. It's a shame, right?'

Not looking for a debate, the guy from Depok answered curtly, 'Oh yeah, really? I just don't think I could handle it.'

'Well if that's the case, find yourself a lady who can handle it for you,' Amran said.

'What do you mean?'

'If the lady's faith is strong, I'm sure she'd be willing to give alms.'

'So these ladies will pay our way?' asked the guy from Depok, realising that Amran had a different interpretation of 'handling it' than he'd intended.

'Yeah, I'm sure it's no problem, we worship together, am I right?'

Amran then launched into a lengthy spiel about the virtues of wealthy women willing to pay alms. He only had one wife so far, but that was just because he hadn't yet been blessed with prosperity. He said there was a dentist who his wife had chosen to be his second wife. The dentist was ready and willing, didn't mind that Amran was a taxi driver whose monthly income was far below hers. The thing was, approaching D-day, the dentist chose another guy from their community instead. Amran had no hard feelings though, said he was always ready to marry again, anytime.

The taxi pulled up to Coffeewar. The guy from Depok, who'd had his fill of sermons, paid and got out, but not without first hearing Amran's closing exhortation to get ready to fulfil his religious obligations wholly and thoroughly.

The music at Coffeewar ended at 11pm. Our beloved guy from Depok was ready to head home. The coffeeshop owner, however, detained him. 'I want to chat,' he said. He knew this would mean having to listen to the Coffeewar owner bad mouth the brilliant manager José Mourinho for at least half an hour, followed by another 40 minutes of expounding on (and huffing and puffing about) why his beloved football club, Arsenal, had been consistently cursed with bad luck for years and years on end.

'Arsène Wenger, now there's a great coach,' said the coffee shop owner. Like millions of other Arsenal fans throughout the world, he had the astonishing fortitude of the Jews living under the Pharoah's rule in Egypt thousands of years ago.

'Yeah, great when he was in Japan,' our beloved guy from Depok retorted.

'You're a real asshole, ya know that?'

They laughed.

Usually, when the guy from Depok paid a visit to Coffeewar, the owner would graciously offer to give him a ride home, since he lived in Lenteng Agung. He would often drive him to Jalan Margonda, sometimes even all the way to his home in

Depok Dua Tengah. Perhaps this generosity was his way of atoning after inundating the guy from Depok with Arsenal mythology. That night, however, the coffee shop owner was going to sleep at his in-laws' place in Kemayoran because his wife and kids were staying there. At one in the morning, the guy from Depok ordered a cab.

As the guy from Depok sat down in the passenger seat, the driver asked if he had the address and passenger's name correct. The guy from Depok, who was getting sleepy again, nodded.

'Was it your wife who ordered the cab?' asked the taxi driver.

The guy from Depok, who deep down was a friendly sort, forced a smile to his lips. Another misunderstanding on account of his ambiguous first name. 'I ordered the cab myself, that's my name,' he said.

'Because ya know, it'd be a shame if it was a woman ordering a cab, so late at night.'

'What are you talking about?'

'The operator didn't mention the destination. I thought, ya know, because it's a woman ordering, poor thing, even if it were a short distance, I'd still drive her.'

'You don't take pity on men?'

'It's a taxi driver's duty, isn't it, Pak?'

Two minutes passed without conversation. The guy from Depok who had gone to Jakarta in the morning and was now on his way home late at night read the ID on the dashboard: Jimmy Zulkifli.

'You have a cool name, Pak Jimmy, where you from?'

'Jambi. But my friends down at the depot call me Jimin. Javanese guys, ya know. It's hard for them to say "Jimmy",' Jimmy replied, laughing heartily at his gibe.

'Where in Jambi? Kota Jambi or Kuala Tungkal?'

'Jambi,' said Jimmy.

'Is the Batang Hari still clean?' the guy from Depok asked, beginning to feel like his seat was kind of warm.

'Uh… I've never been. My dad's from Jambi, mom's from Java,' Jimmy replied.

Three minutes passed without conversation. Jimmy steered toward Pasar Minggu.

'Why not just go straight through Buncit?' the guy from Depok asked.

'It's a shortcut.'

'But it'll take longer.'

'Nah, nah, it won't take longer.'

The taxi got held up for seven minutes near the market. Arriving at the intersection to turn south, Jimmy smiled. 'It's practical, right? From here we just go straight. If we went through Buncit, we'd have to circle back again to Ranco. It'd be a shame for the passenger, ya know, it's too far.'

Another minute passed without conversation.

'You own the café back there?' Jimmy asked.

'No, it belongs to my friend.'

'Is your friend an army man?'

'No.'

'I was thinking, ya know, because the parking attendant was a big guy, he was even wearing an army jacket. What was he, special forces?' asked Jimmy.

'No.'

'What kind of drinks they got there?'

'All kinds, mostly coffee.'

'Is it expensive?'

'It's average, for what you get. I think a cup's around 25,000 rupiah.'

'Wow, I can't afford that. Price like that include milk?'

'Yeah, if you like.'

'Wild horse milk?'

'Any kind of milk, as long as it's wild,' answered the guy

from Depok, who, though getting sleepier, felt the urge to joke around.

Jimmy Zulkifli laughed hard and long. He seemed truly amused by the guy from Depok's joke.

'What do you do for a living, Pak?' Jimmy asked.

'I design parks and gardens.'

'You know Gepeng Srimulat?'[4]

'Wait, what does that have to do with anything?' the guy from Depok responded.

'You're a funny guy. I want to tell that one to my friends at the depot. "Any kind of milk, as long as it's wild," hahaha.'

Jimmy Zulkifli proceeded to list off anything and everything that crossed his mind between the words 'milk' and 'wild.' Some of it inappropriate to repeat here. After finishing his list, Jimmy laughed a satisfied laugh.

'Anyway, where'd Pak Jimmy work before driving a cab?'

'On a ship.'

Jimmy went on to name a few countries that he'd visited in his time as a sailor, Argentina being one of them.

'Wow, awesome, all the way to Argentina. Is it cold there?'

'Well, ya know, when it's the season,' Jimmy said, as if starting to feel bad for his passenger.

'If you're not careful, you could get lost and wind up at the North Pole, right?'

'Impossible. It's not like we used a stick to find the way, ya know. We got compasses, fax machines…'

The look in Jimmy's eyes displayed an increasing sense of pity for his passenger. It was as if, at some point in the past he'd met someone whom he'd thought was the biggest bozo in the world, and now, with this guy from Depok, he'd found someone twice as dumb. Meanwhile, our beloved guy from Depok couldn't figure out how a fax machine could help you navigate a boat; but, unfortunately, his mind soon shifted back to imagining the hopeless looks on his professors' faces when he still couldn't intelligently answer basic questions about cartography when trying, for the third time, to pass his final exam.

Another three minutes passed without conversation. The taxi passed Margo City on Jalan Margonda. In about fifteen minutes it would arrive at the guy from Depok's home.

'How old are you?' asked Jimmy.

'Forty-eight. I turn forty-nine at the end of the year.'

'Wow, no grey hairs, huh?'

The guy from Depok wondered how Jimmy could possibly know the colour of his hair. But he answered anyway, 'Well, I have a few. But my hair's thinning.'

'I'm fifty-one, but my hair's all grey from eating too much Indomie,' said Jimmy.

If Jimmy hadn't mentioned instant noodles there was a strong chance that the guy from Depok whose hair was thinning would have repeated the words of Woody Allen from the opening scene of *Annie Hall*, which, more or less, state that there are two ways for men to age: your hair thins and then turns grey or your hair turns grey and then thins, what's certain is that it'll all be gone for both of them. But because he hadn't anticipated Jimmy's response, all he could ask was, 'Who told you that?'

'The doctor, Pak,' Jimmy said.

'What doctor?'

'The doctor that's always on the radio, Pak. So if you eat Indomie make sure you wash it first, so that your hair doesn't all turn grey like mine.'

The taxi pulled up to our beloved guy from Depok's home. He paid and got out.

'Pak, remember my number. I'll drive you again another time,' Jimmy said.

'Alrighty!'

Talking with Jimmy, not to mention the long day he'd had, made the guy from Depok who was once taken for a Japanese tourist's head spin. That night, for the very first time, he could truly empathise with what Vitalstatistix went through in that *Asterix and the Chieftain's Shield* issue: intellectual exhaustion. After washing up, the guy from Depok was ready to head off to sleep. All of a sudden he remembered. He had to go back to the US Embassy with his passport in just a few hours and wouldn't be able to sleep that night either.

Notes

1. In Indonesia, it is customary to use Pak, Bapak or Saudara to address men and Bu, Saudari or Ibu to address women. Pak and Bapak are literally translated as 'father', the later being more formal.
2. Habib, 'meaning beloved' or 'most loved', is an honorific to address descendants of the Prophet Muhammad, who lived in the Hadhramaut valley, Yemen; Southeast Asia; and the Swahili Coast, East Africa. However, in Indonesia, not all who bear the title are descendants of the prophet.
3. Ilmu is used to refer to knowledge of any sort, and particular scientific knowledge.
4. Gepeng was an Indonesian comedian who became famous in the 1980s.

About the Editors

Maesy Ang and Teddy W. Kusuma run POST, an independent bookshop and publisher based in a traditional market in Jakarta. POST Bookshop champions titles from Indonesian independent publishers and curated titles in English. In its first six years, the bookshop has hosted over 300 events, from writing classes and zine workshops, to book discussions and readings. Its publishing arm, POST Press, has released a handful of titles ranging from novellas to children's literature – three of which have been published internationally. Their first fiction title, *Semasa*, was published in 2018.

About the Authors

Sabda Armandio is a novelist, short story writer, and translator. His first novel, *Kamu*, was published in 2015 and was selected as novel of the year by *Rolling Stone Indonesia*. His other works include a novel, *24 Jam Bersama Gaspar* (24 Hours with Gaspar, 2017), a short story collection, *Kisah-Kisah Suri Teladan* (The Exemplary Tales), and a novella, *Dekat dan Nyaring* (Loud and Close), which was long-listed for the Khatulistiwa Literary Award.

Yusi Avianto Pareanom is a writer, editor, translator, independent publisher, and former journalist. His works of fiction include *Rumah Kopi Singa Tertawa* (The Laughing Lion's Coffee House),

Muslihat Musang Emas (The Golden Fox's Trickery) and *Raden Mandasia si Pencuri Daging Sapi* (Raden Mandasia, the Cow Thief), an award-winning novel that was named one of the books of the year by *Tempo Magazine* and *Rolling Stone Indonesia*. In 2019, he was the Director and Curator of Jakarta International Literary Festival and is currently serving as a member of the Jakarta Arts Council.

Born in West Kalimantan, **Hanna Fransisca** is a poet and short story writer. She has published several collections of short stories and poetry, including *A Man Bathing and Other Poems* (Lontar Foundation). Her first short story, 'My Blood Spills in the Temple', was chosen for the 2008 Jakarta International Literary Festival. She was also named Outstanding Writer by *Tempo Magazine* in 2010 for her collection *Konde Penyair Han* (The Han Poet's Coil). She lives in Jakarta.

Cyntha Hariadi is an award-winning writer and poet. Her work includes the poetry collection, *Ibu Mendulang Anak Berlari* (Mother Feeds, Child Flees), and a collection of short stories entitled *Manifesto Flora* (Flora's Manifesto). Her most recent novel, *Kokokan Mencari Arumbawangi* (Kokokan Seeks Arumbawangi) was published in 2020.

Afrizal Malna (born in Jakarta, 1957) is an Indonesian poet, prose writer, playwright and activist. His poetry collection *Teman-Temanku dari Atap Bahasa* (My Friends from the Roof of Language, 2008) was chosen as the best literary work of 2009 by *Tempo Magazine*. His work has appeared in various publications, including *The Jakarta Post, Horizon, Kompas Daily, Republic, Rule of the People* and *Mind of Representatives*. He has also published two novels, *Novel yang Malas Mengisahkan Manusia* (A Novel Reluctant to Tell of Humans, 2003), and *Lubang dari Separuh Langit* (A Hole from Half the Sky, 2004).

Dewi Kharisma Michellia is a writer working in various genres, from romance, crime, mystery/horror, to sci-fi and fantasy. Her published works include the novel *Surat Panjang tentang Jarak Kita yang Jutaan Tahun Cahaya* (A Long Letter of Our Million Light-Years Distance, 2013) and the short story collection *Elegi* (An Elegy, 2017). In 2015, she co-founded Oak Publisher, an indie publisher based in Yogyakarta, and later in 2018 ran Ruang Perempuan dan Tulisan (Women Writers Space and Writings), a collective dedicated to reading and promoting works by women writers from Indonesia. She is currently reviews editor at *Jurnal Ruang*, an independent news outlet covering books, music, and film.

Ratri Ninditya is a poet and short story writer. Her first poetry collection, *Rusunothing*, was published in 2019. She is also a policy researcher for the Indonesia Arts Coalition.

Ben Sohib was born in 1967 in Jember, East Java. He is a novelist and short story writer, known for his dark humour and focus on the Betawi-Arab community in Jakarta. His work has been adapted for the screen and the film *Tiga Hati, Dua Dunia, dan Satu Cinta* (Three Hearts, Two Worlds, and One Love) won multiple awards at the 2010 Indonesian Film Festival, including best film. His short story collection, *Haji Syiah and Other Stories*, was published by Lontar Foundation in 2015 in a trilingual edition. His most recent work, *Kisah-kisah Perdagangan Paling Gemilang*, was published by Banana in 2020.

utiuts is an entertainment lawyer and a writer. Her first book, *Welcome to the Fandom*, was published in 2019. She lives in Jakarta, Indonesia.

Ziggy Zezsyazeoviennazabrizkie is an Indonesian fiction writer who won the Jakarta Arts Council Novel Writing

Competition for *Di Tanah Lada* (In Pepper Land, 2015), which was later longlisted for Khatulistiwa Literary Award. She won the same competition in 2016 with *Semua Ikan di Langit* (All the Fish in the Sky, 2017), for which she was also awarded the Badan Bahasa Literary Award by the Indonesian Ministry of Education and Culture. Ziggy mainly writes about children and social criticism, both in forms of literary and popular fiction. Her Young Adult novel *Jakarta Sebelum Pagi* (Jakarta Dawning, 2016), was the Editor's Choice Award in *Rolling Stone Indonesia.*

About the Translators

Paul Agusta is a film director, writer, actor and translator. He has made five feature films, as well as several short documentaries and television series. His films have been selected and shown at various international festivals such as International Film Festival Rotterdam, Bucheong Fantastic Film Festival (BiFan), Vancouver International Film Festival, and many more. He is also the co-founder, with Khiva Iskak, of the Bengkel Akting Kuma acting school.

Khairani Barokka is an Indonesian writer and artist. *Modern Poetry in Translation*'s Inaugural Poet-in-Residence, she is Researcher-in-Residence and Research Fellow at UAL's Decolonising Arts Institute, and Associate Artist at the UK's National Centre for Writing. She is co-editor of *Stairs and Whispers: D/Deaf and Disabled Poets Write Back* (Nine Arches), author-illustrator of *Indigenous Species* (Tilted Axis), and author of debut poetry collection *Rope* (Nine Arches Press). Her next book is *Ultimatum Orangutan* (Nine Arches, 2021).

Shaffira D. Gayatri is an Indonesian translator. She holds an MA in World Literature from the University of Warwick, and her translations from Indonesian to English have been published in *Asymptote Journal, Kill Your Darlings,* and the anthology *The Near and The Far, Volume 2.*

Mikael Johani is a poet, critic, and translator in Jakarta. His works have appeared in *#UntitledThree, On Relationships, Asymptote, The Johannesburg Review of Books, AJAR, Vice, Kerja Tangan* and *Popteori.* He is the author of the poetry collection *We Are Nowhere And It's Wow* (POST Press, 2017). He runs Paviliun Puisi, Jakarta's biggest spoken word night.

Zoë McLaughlin is a writer, translator, and librarian. She was a Shansi fellow at Gadjah Mada University in Yogyakarta, Indonesia and a Darmasiswa scholar at the Indonesian Institute of Arts, Surakarta, where she studied classical Javanese dance. She was also an American Literary Translation Association mentee.

Daniel Owen is a poet, translator, and editor. His translation from the Indonesian of Afrizal Malna's *Document Shredding Museum* was published in Australia in 2019 by Reading Sideways Press, and other translations (of work by Malna and Farhanah) have been published in *The Poetry Project Newsletter, Asymptote, Exchanges, Jacket2, A Perfect Vacuum, The Brooklyn Rail,* and elsewhere. He is the author of the poetry books *Toot Sweet* (United Artists, 2015) and *Restaurant Samsara* (Furniture Press, 2018). He edits and designs books and participates in many processes of the Ugly Duckling Presse editorial collective.

Rara Rizal is the co-founder of translators' collective In Other Words. She is also an interpreter and a poet. Her home will always be Pangkep, but she has come to love Jakarta.

Annie Tucker is an LA-based writer and translator. Her translation of Eka Kurniawan's *Beauty is a Wound* was one of *New York Times'* notable books of the year and won the 2016 World Reader's Award.

Syarafina Vidyadhana is a translator, interpreter, and poet based in Jakarta. In 2016, she helped establish POST Press, and served as art director and editor until 2019. She is the curator and editor of *Vice Indonesia*'s speculative fiction special edition, 'Indonesia 2038' (2018). These days she runs a translators' collective In Other Words, and is working on what may just be her debut poetry collection.

Eliza Vitri Handayani is an internationally published writer of fiction and nonfiction. She writes in Indonesian and English. Her novel *From Now On Everything Will Be Different* was published by Vagabond Press in 2015. Her short fiction and essays have appeared in *The Griffith Review, Asia Literary Review, Exchanges Journal, Index on Censorship* and *The Jakarta Post* among others. She is also the founder and director of InterSastra, a platform for literary and artistic exploration and exchange.